I0535603

A Kiss to Keep You

Rebel Wayfarers MC
#9.25

MariaLisa deMora

Edited by Hot Tree Editing

First Published 2016

ISBN 13: 978-0-9983267-0-2

DEDICATION

All that we see or seem,
Is but a dream within a dream. – Edgar Allen Poe

For everyone who has courageously breached their own internal walls and let in the world. Look at you go, you brave thing you. Rock on. You're my hero.

CONTENTS

ACKNOWLEDGMENTS

To be born and live in interesting times is said to be a curse. I would rather think of it as an opportunity to be one of the game changers. Those folks who manage, by virtue of their own stubbornness and effort, to make a worthy difference in the world.

Brute, from *A Kiss to Keep You*, I believe has traits of one of those people. The ones who breathe life into those interesting times. I love how he quietly sets things right in his world, in this story as well as others to come, and I have enjoyed watching the ripples of those efforts expand in growing circles of influence until there's no end to the good things he's set into motion.

That's one of the things I want to do with this story. Ripples of real influence. For the first year of publication, half of all royalties earned from sales of this title will go to a charity of my choice. At the time of this writing, I am still settling the details, but my selection will benefit USA military veterans.

My dad was a proud career Air Force serviceman. I learned that pride from him, absorbed it into my soul, and have a deep-seated respect and love for our military. Daddy was a boom operator on a KC135 refueling jet and flew during the Cuban Missile Crisis, the Korean Conflict, and the Vietnam War. He rode motorcycles, and once rode his bike from the boom operator school in California back home to northeast Texas. That man had stories for days. Miss him all the time.

This novella is about a soldier who was severely wounded while deployed overseas. As part of my research for the book I had conversations with a number of combat-wounded veterans to get a sense of how they dealt with their various injuries, and what the reaction was from folks back home. I learned that the struggles they face in their day-to-day lives are profound, and I want to do something that can make a difference.

For now, I'm still on the hunt for a charity I can get behind. One that supports veterans at a local level, whatever local is to that group. One my daddy would believe in. I'll report in as things develop. I'm excited about the opportunities that have opened up, as well as the connections I've made throughout this process.

This section is always about the thank yous that I owe folks. They are multitude, as ever, because no way can these books happen just with me.

Keith, Nick, Thomas, and Ramone, thank you for your generous time and kind words. Your service to our country is priceless, and I am forever grateful to you.

Becky Johnson and the Hot Tree Editing beta readers, you help make me sound so much smarter than I truly am. Thanks for that!

Dyana Newton, because when I messaged you about describing a burn and blast victim using words like "grafts and therapy" and how to "minimize scars turning keloid and hypertropic" you took the time to talk me through some difficult scenes, and gave me the real scoop on how things would be handled, thank you.

My alpha readers and critique partners: Jamey, MirandaPanda, Kori, and Megan – y'all rock hard. Thank you for your patience with me.

Thanks also to Lila Rose, for helping me get some Aussie in my story. You are one of my favorite people in life. Love me some Lila.

I've heard from readers how some folks look avidly for these letters I slip into the beginning of my stories and books. How you can get a sense of how the story will unfold. In this, the last story I'll publish in 2016, the year I promised to be consciously wooful in my writing, I hope you find it full of the woo that we long for.

Woofully yours,
~ML

BRUTE'S GIRL

Brute

He sat on his bike and watched her. Gorgeous, reserved, she seemed unaware of her own beauty, and just as unconscious of his regard, because she never looked up from the book held balanced on her knees. Never raised her gaze to find him watching her. To see the other men in the area looking their fill. Seated on the green grass of the park, back to a tree, she rested with her heels drawn up tight to her bottom while her skirt draped gracefully over her angled legs. With a bottle of water lying nearby, her slouchy messenger bag was tossed to one side, phone nowhere in sight. She had lost herself in the story, as she so often did. Blonde, stunning, and so unattainable, especially for a man like him. She might as well have been on the moon.

Ricky sighed and started his bike, checking traffic before he smoothly pulled out of the lot where he had been sitting for over an hour. The first minutes had been spent anxiously waiting on her arrival, then the remainder, he'd been avidly watching his girl. That was what the guys in the motorcycle club, his brothers, all called her. As he rolled the throttle and accelerated up the street, he was already anticipating the jeering catcalls that would greet him when he pulled into the clubhouse. Brute's Girl.

Gliding the bike to a stop behind traffic, as he waited for the light to turn green, he turned his head, glancing into the car beside him. Without thinking, he smiled fondly at the young girl driving the aged two-door vehicle. She looked a lot like his goddaughter, pert nose covered by freckles, untidy hair tucked behind her ears. Seeing her made him think he needed to call Dylan, see how their Natalie was doing in her first year of college, ask about the family. Then the girl turned her head and saw him. Her reaction was instant and dramatic, hands slapping at the controls on the inside of the door to lock the car, mouth falling open in silent horror. Swiftly, he wiped the smile from his face and turned forward, not wanting to make her more uncomfortable than he already had.

Richard Monte was well acquainted with the societal challenges he had to work within, and around. He should be, he saw evidence of them every time he looked in the mirror. Face mangled by the roadside bomb that had taken most of his patrol, his skin in turns was glossy smooth and cratered from the burns and shrapnel. He knew how the barest glimpse of his countenance could affect those who were unprepared. That was why he

2

didn't go out often; choosing instead to stay in his apartment, his work-from-home job as a help desk technician was without much outside contact. Not content, but merely pragmatic enough to recognize what it did to him every time he provoked a reaction like this one.

The men of the Rebel Wayfarers MC were the exception. Introduced to them by a friend, these people judged him not by what remained of his face, but by his actions and words. Fiercely honorable in their own way, the outlaw group of bikers had folded themselves around him protectively, finding him a job allowing him to support himself. Providing both independence and giving him a community of people he could count on, no matter what.

The girl in the park, the blonde. The beauty he would only ever be able to look at from afar. She was another anomaly in his world. Months ago he had seen her in the grocery store, and she had shocked him by not reacting. Well, not reacting to his face, at least. She had reacted to him as a man, something he hadn't experienced for nearly a decade. Reaching for a boxed dinner, he had clumsily knocked it to the floor, and before he could grab it, the blonde had bent over and picked it up. Holding it behind her back, she had smiled up at him, her tone light and playful as she had asked, "What'll you give me for it?"

Bright blue pools looking right at his face, smile curling her full red lips, cheeks lifted, and that same smile making her eyes fucking dance, she had looked him in the eyes and teased him. Exactly as a woman would do with a man she found attractive. Without hesitation, he'd answered as he would have before the injury, boldly stating the cost. Two words shaping his desires. "A kiss."

Immediately, she'd responded, "Deal," and leaned forward, lifting her chin. Standing there in the grocery store aisle, he had bent slightly, pressing his lips in a brief, soft, closed-mouthed kiss to raspberry-flavored ones. Lips belonging to a beautiful blonde who was curvy but carried it well, cute and knew it, standing close to him in a strapless sundress still swinging slightly around her calves.

When he'd pulled back, she'd held the pose for a moment, lashes a shade darker than her hair resting on her cheeks, lips slightly parted, an adorable flush rising in her cheeks. Then her blue eyes had opened, and she again looked at him without distaste or fear, no cringing or hesitation in her appearance. "Here's your box," she'd murmured, and he'd reached for the container. She'd handed it over but had stayed in place for a moment, then an expression of regret had flashed across her features before she'd said, "See you around." Ricky had stood there watching as she'd walked up the aisle away from him, turning to offer him a friendly wave before she'd gone out of sight, the hem of her colorful, swirling skirt the last thing he saw.

He had abandoned his cart in the store to follow her outside, noting the make and model of her car. Then, like the sad sack he was, he'd stalked her all the way to her house on the outskirts of town. He had been surprised to find she didn't live too far from his apartment, only four blocks. Rare beauty, and so close to hand. Her house a tiny cottage tucked in alongside family homes in a well-established neighborhood, an oddness for the area. A generation ago it was probably used as a mother-in-law's residence.

Back at the clubhouse that night, it had been hours later, and he was still turning the encounter over and over in his mind, trying to figure out what had actually happened. It was confusing on many levels. He didn't get flirty anymore. Didn't get sweet. Sure didn't get kissed in public exposed under the too-bright lights of a grocery store.

One of the guys had plied him with booze and then worked to pry the story out of him. That was when she got her name. They already called him Brute, a plain statement of his looks but one that held surprisingly little sting, because it wasn't done maliciously, but supportively. His looks didn't matter to them, and the name they dubbed him with was a way for them to show it. So Brute's Girl, well, that just came naturally.

Since then he had watched her. He didn't think she had caught sight of him again. Probably harbored no memory of the gift she had given him, but oh, how he watched her.

Watched her go out with her friends, always their designated driver. Sticking close, never ditching them for a man, even if plenty of men approached her. Watched her go to work at the salon where she chatted and laughed, hands buried in the hair of men and women who sat in her chair. Where she made already pretty people beautiful. She had family in town, and he'd watched her play in the yard of her brother's house, pounding a fist into the worn leather pocket of a glove. She'd called encouragingly to her nephew as she returned his throws to her, ball after ball, the boy seeming to tire of their game long before she did.

Those were her social moments, and she acted entirely comfortable in any situation. She had good friends who she looked out for, work she appeared to love, and she seemed tight with her family. A good life. A real one she had created herself.

But she wasn't afraid to be alone, either. She read all the time, and he watched her in the library, strolling up and down the stacks, fingertips dragging along the spines of the books as if she couldn't bear to not touch them. He followed her into theaters, trailing in behind her only after the film started, a point when he could be certain her attention would be on the feature. Alone in a seat halfway back, on the aisle, she was easy to find, his view of her by the flickering reflections from the screen no less satisfying than the bright sunlight of the park. Dinners out by herself. Sometimes with a book in hand, at times watching the people around her, not afraid of solitary entertainment. Him on the bike staking out the lot, watching from whatever vantage point that allowed him to see her table.

He watched, watched all the time, but didn't approach. Mostly because he couldn't figure her out. Her behavior in the grocery store seemed at odds with everything he knew about women, but the more he learned about her, the more it seemed in line with what she would do. See something she wanted and go after it, full steam ahead. Unafraid. Even of him, looking the way he did, nightmare features fixed forever in place on his face. In this scenario, the only anomaly was him.

He kept an eye on her, and because he liked what he saw, he helped where he could. When her lawnmower had broken, evidenced by the length of the grass growing in the yard, he'd fixed it. It wasn't hard, just adjusting a cable. Took all of five minutes, him walking from a block away and then crouched in the shadows of her garage, retreating once he was done. Leaving the repaired mower on the walk between her garage and house where she couldn't miss it, he'd affixed a note explaining what had happened and how she could prevent it in the future.

She had retrieved the note, untying the stiff card from the handle and standing in the yard. She'd studied it for long minutes, turning it this way and that to find nothing more than the straightforward lines of printed writing. She'd remained in place for a beat, then two before looking up and glancing around, not seeing him tucked behind one of the houses half a block away. Head down and still studying the note, she had walked into the house, where she and the note had disappeared.

When her car had needed brakes, the chirping of the pads a loud indication their replacement should be attended to, he'd arranged for a fake giveaway prize to be delivered to her at the salon. The hundred dollars for maintenance was at a nearby garage known for a variety of things, one of which was good brake work. Ricky was there when she'd arrived, he'd seen her drive in and talk to Don, the shop owner and his friend. Don had come out of the office, leaving her behind—seated in a cracked plastic chair, curvy legs crossed at the knee, magazine in hand—and he'd nodded at Ricky who'd made quick work of zipping up his coveralls and rolling himself underneath the car. It gave him a great deal of satisfaction to be the one to fix things for her. Big things, little things, it didn't really matter, he just liked knowing he made her life a little easier.

With her focus on everyone except herself, she needed someone to watch out for her. Brute could do that. Do that for her. Do that for him. Take on that role and safeguard her, like he'd want someone to watch out for his goddaughter, Natalie, away at school and by herself.

Now, sitting at a light alongside a girl who was horrified just by looking at him, he snorted. Sure, he could be a fairy godfather. Right.

BEXLEY

She woke slowly, already nauseated before she even failed at lifting her pounding head from the mattress. *Crap.* She took a measured, shallow breath, knowing from long-ago experiences that breathing too deeply would only worsen the sick feeling roiling in her stomach. Since lifting her head didn't work, she rolled her aching eyes side to side to ascertain she was, indeed, in her own bed. Okay. Home. That was good. That was normal, because she never woke up not at home.

Clenching her teeth against the pain, she shifted on the mattress, freezing in place when she realized she was entirely undressed. Naked. Literally bare as the day she was born, it didn't feel like she had a stitch of clothing on her body. *Crap.* That was not good, and definitely not normal.

Focusing intently, she ran an inventory of her body, trying to determine without movement, if there were any...select areas that hurt. Head, well, yeah, this was a hell of a hangover. Worst she'd ever had, so pain there, check. Shoulders and arms, no. Breasts and belly, no. Skip the middle for now. Toes and feet, legs and knees, no pain. Clenching her eyes even more tightly shut, she paid attention to her thighs and the area of her groin where they joined her body. No aching, no throbbing. Just naked. Good, but not good, still better than bad.

Rolling her head slowly to one side, she opened one eye just a slit, looking at the nightstand where she usually plugged in her phone. Secure in the holder that attached it to the speakers in the room, the clock face showed her it was early, not quite eight o'clock. Good. She opened her other eye the same small slit and realized the time was actually evening. So very not good.

She had seemingly been unconscious for an entire day. Verifying the date, she closed her eyes, relieved it was Sunday and the only day of the week she didn't book official appointments. If it had been Monday, even as light as that day usually was with folks headed back to work, she would have had some apologizing to do to clients who didn't get their cut and color in when they scheduled it. Sunday was her day off, had been since she started officially doing hair after earning her certification.

She didn't mind doing family on a Sunday, usually just a trim when her boys would be getting shaggy, and she would take care of it in the family's kitchen, sheet or towel clothespinned around the neck of her victim. Just like when she and Brice were kids back in Oregon, when she'd trimmed his hair with fabric shears because their parents didn't have the cash or inclination to make sure it got done. Her older brother liked his place on the baseball and football teams, and the coach, shared between the sports, wanted his boys clean-cut. She made sure Brice stayed that way so he could keep his happy spot playing on the fields, and not grumping because he was riding the pine. That meant this being Sunday, what could have been a terrible crap day, was just crap.

Because her brain was so fuzzy, it took her working through all that in her head before she realized she had seen something other than her phone on the nightstand. That something made her tense up, which made the sick roll through her system again until she clenched her jaw on the raw sounds bubbling up her burning throat. Swallowing bitter bile, she battered at it until it subsided, then she opened her eye a fraction, focusing on what was beside the phone.

A tall glass, half full of what looked like water. Large, square ice cubes floated in the clear liquid, and condensation was gathering on the sides of the glass. As Bexley watched, a couple of the drops collected, flowing together to form a larger drop. It then trailed a meandering line down the side of the glass which was sitting on a folded paper napkin, the edges of the square crisp, straight folds lined up with the sides of the tabletop. Next to the napkin were two small, round, white tablets, an unmistakable logo pressed into the surface. She knew the brand, and also knew she didn't have it in the house, because the ones she used were

11

formed into oblongs. Water. Fresh, cold, ice water. Painkillers.

She mentally scanned her body again, paying very close attention to specific areas a second time, but came up with the same answer. No. She had, thankfully, most emphatically *not* gotten stupid in addition to wasted. Staring at the glass, she revised that assessment. She had gotten wasted because she had apparently brought someone home with her and didn't have any memories of that event. But, given the care evidenced by the water and aspirin, not stupid wasted because the person she'd brought home gave a crap.

She heard sounds coming from inside the house and shifted her focus to those, hating how fuzzy she felt, wanting to be sharp, on it. Wanted to be on her game and able to take care of herself, but instead she was flat on her back on her bed, not even able to pick up her own head without barfing. It wasn't a large house. She didn't need large, with no pets, no husband, no kids, but it had what she did need, which was a location blazingly close to her brother, Brice, and his son, Duncan.

She needed that, because they were why she was here.

After her sister-in-law, Jean, died in a stupid, senseless accident—knocked off a sidewalk by a couple in the throes of an altercation, the shouting match turning to shoving, and Jean, an innocent victim, had been thrust into the path of oncoming traffic—Bexley moved here to Fort Wayne. Picked up and moved without hesitation, because after that had happened, there was no way she was going to stay all the way across the country from the only family she claimed. The pain and sorrow running through Brice's voice when he'd called her to tell her about Jean had scored deep. It scored deeper, finding out about him holding back half the story. Protecting her by waiting until she arrived in town to let her in on the fact that Duncan, then barely two years old, had sat alone, sleeping peacefully in a stroller on the sidewalk while everyone focused on the tangled and twisted mass of flesh that was his mother. Alone. Sleeping, but more on his own than any child should ever be, at two years old or twenty. Alone, and frighteningly vulnerable.

It had been hours before Brice got the call about Jean.

It would be hours more before anyone put two and two together who the abandoned child was. That entire time Brice had been going out of his mind at the hospital. Hours with no answers, just a growing fear that he'd lost his entire family. Minutes ticking past while he'd been on his own, alone and grieving, crazed with worry. Then at the police station, a dozen officers surrounding him with compassionate understanding but little help. It terrified her that he'd been so alone, vulnerable.

Duncan's predicament had been reported by a store owner who'd carefully watched the stroller before wheeling it through his door and making a call. It was a savvy social worker who'd eventually realized that the boy hadn't been abandoned, but was with the woman killed in a pedestrian versus auto accident where her shoes were halfway up the block, and her body at the intersection beyond that. Her son left behind, stroller angled away from the street by the force of her hands knocked from the handles.

Fortunately for Bex, her chosen career allowed her to pick up and go wherever, as long as she could pass the state's registration and certification process for cosmetology. That meant she could leave the mild but wet clime of Portland where she had been living at the time and head to Fort Wayne, where her brother had settled because it was where Jean's family lived. The state had a thing for basketball, but loved their football, too, so it had felt about half home to him already, Jean bringing that other half to his house.

So Bex's little cottage of a house in a pleasant Fort Wayne neighborhood didn't matter a bit to her, except that it gave her the essentials. A roof that Duncan could stay underneath as needed, parking for her car, because she seriously hated scraping ice off her windows and if anyone thought Indiana only had snow, they were nuts. It also was only two blocks from Brice's place and gave her access to public transportation, which provided the option of bussing it to work in bad weather. The furniture pieces were all mismatched, but functional, yard sale finds and looked it, but she wasn't house proud. No, she kept her most precious things closer, on display. School papers sporting a red A+ held with magnets to the front of the refrigerator, picture portraits framed in a cheesy collage with six empty spaces still to fill, room for Duncan's high school career.

The sounds came nearer, and she called out, shocked at how raspy her voice sounded. Dry and painful coming out, the single word apparently had the power to stop the footsteps from coming closer. "Hello?" Silence greeted her, and she strained her ears to listen, trying hard to hear anything, wanting to be prepared when whoever came through the doorway, because she had no memories of last night. Zero retention of whatever smashing party she had gotten smashed at.

"Hello?" Her voice didn't sound any better a second time, and she wondered what time her helper had poured her into bed, knowing there was no way she'd put herself here, because she never, as in nev-*er* slept naked. Not with the chance Brice would need her for something with Duncan, and both of her boys having keys which meant they didn't have to knock when they wanted in her house.

Finally, another noise, this sounding from the wall right outside her room, as if something had leaned against it, no longer approaching, but holding in place. Then a voice. It was amazing; full of gravel and rougher than even hers was, new but sounding strangely familiar. She'd never known a voice could be gentle, but this one was, gently asking her, "How's the head?"

"Like the time I earned a baseball bat thrown at me by my best friend in sixth grade, all because I told a boy she wanted to kiss him." *Jesus*, she thought, *that was stupid. I coulda just said that it hurt. I didn't have to give part of a story long forgotten*.

"Taking that to mean she connected." Still rough and jagged, the voice held tender humor threading through it. Without knowing why, Bexley smiled.

15

"She was our pitcher, and we played fastball, not drop pitch." *Another answer without answering, I just get better and better.*

"So, prolly had an accurate eye, and I suspect she let it fly, so a hard hit." A definite chuckle followed that statement, and she rolled her eyes, wincing as they ached even more. That chuckle was worth working for, and she decided she wanted to see what went with the chuckle and voice, so she could work for another one.

"Yeap." Bex cleared her throat. "Could you come all the way in here? I think I need to thank you. I'm probably the worst pickup in the history of pickups, if you're the one who left me the meds."

"You aren't a fucking pickup." This emphatic response was immediate and sounded snarled, and she felt a buzz of anger that swelled from the hallway to land deep in her bones. A feeling which set her stomach to shaking. Not all her boyfriends had been nice, and one of them in particular frequently gave off a vibe that made her stomach quake like this, so she knew her reaction for what it was. *Fear*. Aware she was alone, vulnerable and naked, her breathing grew shallow, nearly a pant.

She realized he could hear her when he spoke, his voice softly susurrant, quieting her fears without words. "Shhhhhh." Noise, him shifting against the wall, and for a moment, she thought he would come inside. "I'd never hurt you."

"I…" She swallowed. "I didn't…." The fear subsided slowly, nausea rolling in its wake.

16

His voice came again, softer but still with a rough edge when he asked, "Think you can keep down the aspirin?"

"If I..." Bex realized her voice had fallen to a near-silent whisper. Pausing, she cleared her throat, earning her another shot of pain in her head, making her wince as she said, "If I could reach it, maybe, but the way I feel, honestly...probably not."

"*Fuck.*"

She tried to push past that ball of fear in her belly, wanted him to know she wasn't without resources. Wanted to thank him not just for taking care of her, but for taking care with her. *Shhhhhh. I'd never hurt you.* "If you could just come in so I can thank you, you could hand me my phone. You don't have to stay. You've done enough already. Very kind. I'll call my brother. He lives just—"

"He's at Duncan's game." He interrupted her brusquely, and a second later she heard footsteps receding down the hall. The voice decreased in volume with each spoken syllable. He was leaving. "You're talkin'. You're good. I'm out. You'll be fine."

Sounds of boot soles on bare wood slapped the walls, descending the stairs. "Hello?" Back to her questioning call, she waited, then listened, shocked, as the backdoor opened then closed. Silence descended upon her house again, broken only by her disbelieving restatement of what the man had said. "He's at Duncan's *game*?"

BRUTE

Fuck.

He should have left when she'd eased from her unresponsive drugged state to a healthier sleep. He shouldn't have waited. But even before that, he should not have undressed her. Should not have bathed her, washing evidence of the night from her body. Should not have watched her sleep, that sleep restless unless his hand was touching her. Should not have lain on the bed beside her, alert to every movement, gaze captured by her profile, the shifting of her eyes underneath their lids. Cataloging the tiny winces that gave away her rise to consciousness, which drove him to her kitchen, the bags on his bike, and then back to her room with items in hand to make her day more comfortable. Fuck, he should have left after he dropped the glass and pills on her table.

He should not have stayed.

But he had.

Should not have done any of those things.

But after seeing how close she came to being...destroyed, he couldn't not.

So he did.

Brute dug a phone from his pocket, tapped on the screen a few times, got an answering buzz accompanying a text response and shoved the phone back into his pocket. As he knew they would, his brothers had his back last night, and there was a present waiting for him in the clubhouse basement.

He took a deep breath, then started the bike, idling out of the alley behind her cottage and onto the street, not opening the throttle until he was well away from her neighborhood. He wasn't in any specific hurry. He grinned, the movement of his lips pulling the skin of his face tight in grotesque ways. This particular present wasn't going to get up and walk away.

***

"I'm gonna want verbal affirmation that we have an understanding." Brute lifted his gaze from the body that sagged in front of him, a dead weight pulling down against the biker holding the man in place, getting an amused snort that did not issue from the person he wanted to hear from.

With a shake of his head, Gunny released the man. "Not thinkin' you're gonna get shit out of him for fifteen, brother."

"What in the…I didn't hit him that hard." He hadn't either. "Pulled every punch."

"Yeah, but we dosed him with what he hit your gal with. A big dose. So, however bad she's feeling today, he's got it three times worse." Gunny leaned back, shoulders against the wall. "She make it through okay?"

Gunny had seen her, one of only a few of the men who had, the ones Brute relied on to have his back. Gunny knew what Brute had found in the girl, wanted it for him. Wanted to see it taken through to culmination. So Gunny spent time arguing, and had reasoned and debated unsuccessfully with Brute about keeping his distance.

But Gunny didn't live behind his face; Brute did. He knew, if he had stepped foot inside that bedroom two hours ago with her awake and probably already worried about who was in her house with her, she would have lost her mind with fear. From her words, her voice, her fucking breathing—he knew she was already terrified. He couldn't have blamed her, but it would have cut him deep, spoiling the illusion that he had one woman in this world who didn't flinch at the sight of him. One woman who could be his. Would have ruined the memory of her lips under his in bright, illuminating light.

She was his singular dream. Spectacular in his experience, and he wanted to hold onto that for as long as he could. That moment in the store with her teasing smile promising more. Promising everything to him with a lift of her eyes to his. His for the taking. She was everything. Not a stupid skank drilled from behind in a dark room, his friends careful to take phones away, not letting any light into the space. She was Bexley. Brute's Girl.

Last night when she'd gone out alone, he'd followed.

By the light affixed to her back wall, he could see her dress was casual: running shoes, jeans, and a tee, covered with a leather jacket. This was a break from her regular routine. She went out to party, but always with her friends, which meant clubs and club clothes. When she went out, she dressed to impress, taking the up route, not dressing down.

He didn't like the feeling this gave him, so he watched. She walked around to the front of the house and stood for about a minute before a cab showed, her long legs and rounded curves folding into the backseat. Following closely, knowing the driver wouldn't be watching for him, he stayed within a couple of car lengths of the vehicle, trailing it to a bar on the east side of town. A village long ago annexed by the city, they stopped in front of a building just off the main drag, not a place you would even know about unless you were from there. The kind of place populated by patrons from the neighborhood, those established regulars inhabiting their self-assigned stools, jukebox still old school, spinning actual records, selection limited to the faded paper in the flipping display on the front. His kind of place. A little dingy, a lot dark, entirely low class and comfortable holding that position.

Not her kind of place.

The cab pulled up by the front walk and a few seconds later, she exited, moving directly to the entrance as if she made this trip every night. Door open and closed, and he was left sitting on his bike in an adjacent parking lot, empty sidewalk and blank walls spread in front of him. No windows, no vantage point, no eyes on her.

Three minutes later, he had parked by the backdoor and was prowling through the kitchen, snapping, "Not if you know what's good for you," at the single worker who had balls enough to start to say something. The man was also smart enough to know when to shut up, and Brute parked himself just inside the swinging pass-through where he could look out a diamond-shaped glass set head-high in the door. Bevels along the edge warped his view of the room, but it was still clear enough he could see her.

Seated at the bar, forearms leaning in, she looked at home, as if she had perched this way every night for the past decade, having celebrated her majority here. He watched her joke with the bartender, a good-looking man about her age.

Without turning to look, Brute motioned behind his back to the kitchen, hearing the pause in movement across the entirety of the room before one set of footsteps came closer. "Tell me about the barman."

The young voice coming from his elbow let him associate it with a face noted during his walk-through scan. The dishwasher boy had been the only one with curiosity enough to approach. Brute kept his eyes on the bartender, listening as the kid snorted quietly. "Kasmouski. Mouse."

"He worked here long?" Brute tensed as the gal went through one shot of vodka, then another, Mouse standing close with the bottle for an amused moment, waiting to pour a third which she left sitting on the bar. Mouse placed an ice water on the counter in front of her with a smile. She dug into her pocket, pulling out a doubled-over bundle of bills, chatted with the barman for another moment before peeling off two from the middle, creasing them in half lengthwise to make them easier to pick up off the bar and slid the money across to where he stood.

Brute could read her lips when she told the man, "I'm good," turning down his offer to get her change. Not a stranger to bars, then. Not a stranger to being a stranger in a bar, either. There were unspoken rules that made it so people who wanted to fold seamlessly into new places could create a space for themselves, even at neighborhood bars like this. Stay off tab until the bar help knows you. Demonstrate you have the cash to cover your evening and are confident enough to give a little show. Make it easy for them to scoop the money, so they look slick doing it. They appreciate each gesture, gives them a reason to ensure you stayed lubricated. Tip the bartender early and well and you would not be a patron allowed to go dry. They would learn your name and use it, handing back that feeling of belonging in exchange.

"Few years. Longer than me." The kid spoke again, and Brute frowned down, feeling a body get close, crowding his space so the boy could lift to his toes and look through the glass. "If she's your woman, you don't have to worry about Mouse." These words set Brute on edge, and he looked again at the bartender, seeing the glint of piercings in both ears, quality clothing even working in this bar. Seeing that, the kid's next statement didn't surprise him. "He's totally gay. Came out to his grandmother and everything. She's cool with it, told him she'd ride as his wingwoman anytime he needed to go out without worrying about anyone having problems."

Brute grunted, and after a minute, he felt the boy wander off, leaving him to his vigil.

For two hours, he watched her nurse that third shot, then a slow fourth and fifth. She would finish a shot and stand, chat for a minute with Mouse, and head to the bathroom, the path taking her out of sight down a hallway that ran the length of the kitchen. From where Brute stood, he could hear the plumbing work, so had eyes on her the instant she cleared the hallway on her way back. Again seated on her stool, she would push the shot glass towards the inner edge of the counter, waiting for the next to be poured before she asked for a fresh glass of water. Smart. Cautious. Not accepting anything that wasn't dispensed in front of her.

So, when the blocky guy came in and wedged himself between her stool and the one next to her, standing, not sitting, it surprised Brute that she didn't push back. Surely she understood a man in her space like that, he had only one thing on his mind, and that thing didn't seem to be what she was looking for.

She had only spoken to Mouse, gracefully shutting down two approaches from other customers by pulling out her phone when she noticed them moving her way. She pretended a conversation, using the mirrors to make sure they saw her chatting and flipping her hair. Doing the kind of things a woman would do when on the phone with her man, making it clear without saying a word that she was taken. Not a little bit, but all the way taken. Which he knew was a flat lie. He had never seen her with a man, or a woman, so it wasn't as if she was a closet Mouse, waiting for the right moment to let her brother know a secret.

She didn't appear to have any secrets that Brute could see. She worked, talked to her friends, spent time alone or with her brother and his son. But she didn't date and didn't do casual hookups, either. So her phone act was just that, an act, and he wondered what in the hell she was doing.

She turned her head, looking up the bar, calling out to Mouse, and Brute saw the blocky guy dig in his pocket, watching the hand that hovered over her still-full shot glass for a moment before returning to that same pocket. The man then moved away without having asked or received anything from the bartender, going now to the jukebox to mess with the screens on the front, punching buttons and flipping the selection descriptions back and forth without playing anything. Brute noted the guy's eyes stayed on her, using the mirror mounted above the juke to watch.

The moment her elbow bent, lifting the glass to her lips, the predator smiled and moved, aggressively pushing to the bar at her side. She glanced up at him, face carefully blank as she sat the shot glass down, then turned back to the bar, taking out her phone and tapping on the screen. That was when Brute got out his phone, calling in a marker with Gunny.

"Right," he told Gunny, pulling his thoughts back to the basement where they stood on either side of the man who'd drugged her. "She made it through okay. Head's hurting, but she's okay."

"She thank you for saving her ass from him?" Gunny used the hard toe of his boot to shove the man in the ribs, grinning as the guy groaned.

"She doesn't remember anything, my guess." Brute glared at the man on the floor. "Roofied like she was, hard to believe anything else. That dose you gave him mean he won't remember this?"

Gunny threw back his head and laughed. "Nope. Gave him that shit hours ago. It's through his system now. Aftereffects, though, those are a bitch. His head's bustin' wide open whether he's here or away, but he's with us when he's awake, brother. This son of a bitch will remember every moment of what you're dealin' out." He toed the man's ribs again, dragging another groan from him. "Once he's cogitatin' again, anyway."

BEXLEY

"So." Brice leaned his head back against the couch cushions, rolling his neck so he could look at her. "You gonna tell me who finally breached the massive and impressive defenses of my sister?"

"What?" Startled, looking down to hide it, she shuffled the popcorn in her bowl, settling the unpopped kernels to the bottom, tossing a few fluffy white morsels into her mouth so her next words were muffled. "Whatchu mean?'

His gaze was on her. She felt the weight of that look as if it were a physical thing because this was one of his favorite topics. She thought that was mostly because he knew it bugged her when he started up with it, so she kept her eyes on the TV, watching the show around the outline of Duncan's head where he sat on the ottoman between the sofa and screen. Brice had loved his wife, loved having that kind of close relationship in his life.

Which meant he hated that Bexley had never found her Jean. Shoot, he had only recently stopped trying to set her up with every single guy he'd met who he'd deemed worthy. Before he could answer, she shouted, "Oh, ugh. Gross, Dunk. Why are we watching this movie again?"

Duncan twisted and looked at her, broad grin in place on his face. "Because zombies are cool, and this show is awesome." He stretched his eyes wide in emphasis as he informed her, "And it's a show, not a movie. This is the first episode. We have tons more to watch." She groaned as he turned back to the TV, his sweet tenor singing out, "Zombie marathon coming up."

"Not sure this is a good idea, Bricey. If he has nightmares, it's on you, Bubba." She flicked another handful of popcorn at her face, picking a couple of missed kernels off her shirt, popping them into her mouth. "When—and I say that with full certainty that I will—when I have nightmares, that's on you, too."

Tone carefully patient, Brice asked, "Who was the guy who answered the phone last Sunday? You know, that day when I called to find out why you didn't make it to Duncan's game? Something you never miss, but skipped on for the first time ever?" Brice hadn't moved, so she knew his gaze was still locked on her.

"What guy?" Dumb was the way to play this, because just telling her brother flat out that she went out to a bar because she was lonely and afraid and wanting to feel something even if that something was terror, was not going to make him happy. Trying to explain that she found herself wanting to spend time in a place where no one knew her because at least then she wasn't *as* lonely, and losing some of that lonely made the rest not seem as bad, was going to make him a lot more *not* happy.

He didn't know and never would know if she maintained her resolve.

Plus, if she told him she thought she'd been drugged while making such a stupid move, he would be even *less* happy than his unhappy butt would already be. Might ask questions, might dig deep if his parent radar pinged. And, if she happened to slip up and tell him that apparently, she had hooked up—she remembered the voice, telling her she wasn't a pickup...no, that wasn't quite right, he told her that she wasn't a *fucking* pickup—and that she had no idea who had answered her phone? Not remembering name or face to go with a voice heard only from the hallway, this while she was flat on her back in bed, *naked*, body clean but soiled clothing soaking in the tub, he would lose his mind with unhappy. To Brice, she was still his little sister, and someone to be protected. So, with no other options, dumb was the only play she had.

"Bex, hon." His voice was pitched low, so Duncan wouldn't hear over the soundtrack of screams coming from the TV speakers. "A man answered your phone. Told me you weren't feeling well. Said he would let you know I was at the game if you needed me." He paused, and she felt the couch shift as he leaned close. "What's your man's name?"

"None of your beeswax." She deliberately used a light tone, laughing as she cut her eyes his way, seeing he was still intent on her. "I'm a grown woman, Bricey. I pick out my own clothes and everything."

"Yeah." He snorted, leaning back into the cushions, head twisting to face the screen. When he spoke again, it was as quiet as before, but the tone was regretful. "I know you are, Bex. I know."

***

She sat on top of the wooden box she pulled out to her postage stamp of a stoop in the summer. Not a porch—the space was not at all large enough for a swing, which she would have *loved*—the stoop could accommodate the box and her legs, but only just with her knees bent and her feet propped on the small wall surrounding one end of the stoop. The box had the advantage of being portable, so when the sun shifted in the late summer, easing around the corner of her house and across the yard in the afternoon, she could adjust where she parked her butt. Piling a thick pillow on the box took it beyond comfortable, and she could lean on an angle against any available wall, keeping all of her people-watching options wide open.

She had been outside about fifteen minutes when it started, a noise heard so frequently over the past months she could almost believe it was coming from a neighbor's garage. Almost, except for the one day when she'd woken up hungover in a way that was memorable and right after she'd heard her backdoor close, she'd heard the noise, and it was close, coming in rolling waves within seconds of the door closing. So close, whatever it was probably sat in her driveway, engine turning over in a rumbling rush. A motorcycle, she had decided. Not a hotrod as she'd first suspected, but a motorcycle.

No cab home for her that night, her mysterious hallway lurker had parked on the cement apron in front of her garage, his walk of shame out in the open for any neighbor to see. So, putting two and two together— something cops didn't seem able to do, but she and social workers had in common—the sound was attached to the man with the unbelievable voice.

That meant she might have some chance of seeing him if he lived nearby. And given the number of times she had heard the sound, she believed—hoped—he had to live close.

She had tried to pinpoint the period in time when she'd started hearing it, but nothing stood out. Nothing around here, anyway. No houses losing their proud realtor "Sold" signs had preceded her first noticing the sound, so maybe he was established. Or maybe had grown up in the neighborhood. The homes on the streets surrounding her were old and most had accommodated families for a long time. Far longer than she had lived here, for sure. What if he'd had to move home, or a parent got sick, or his siblings sold him their portion of inherited childhood memories? What If he was nearby?

Close, but still unseen. And she wanted to see. So now, each time she heard the noise...the engine...the motorcycle, she would begin a stealthy scan of the area, hoping to catch sight of him.

Today would not be her day. Like the last hundred, the rumbling growl quickly died as it moved away, silence settling on the lawn in its wake. *Darn.*

The lawn. Cocking her head, she leaned one shoulder into the corner created where her small entryway joined to the house. Her lawn needed mowing. She would be pulling out her smooth running lawnmower soon, and with every pass across the striped grass, she would remember the note. Careful handwriting that gave nothing away. No swirls or whirls, only straight lines and graceful curves to pass the message of unrequested mechanical assistance. Mysteriously fixed, things set right, then posed in her path without opportunity for a thank you.

With a sigh, she glanced up the sidewalk to see the Sunday morning parade about to begin. First up was the couple from three houses down, pushing a stroller with their twin girls. The worn and comfortable outfits on the toddlers advertising they were headed to the park. Easy parenting there, making sure their little ones only had to focus on the good times, not on rumples and ruffles.

Next was the sister duo, yoked in tandem. Working together to raise the young son of the oldest sibling. They were talking, heads turned to look at the other, laughter welling from their throats as they walked up the sidewalk. Two women, comfortable with the family they'd been given, creating a different unit with their efforts. The boy clasping tight to two pieces of one generation, suspended himself between them, picking his feet up, bent knees twisting, his body swinging wildly back and forth from their strong, supportive hands.

She gave them a wave and a shouted hello, keeping her eyes on them long after they passed her house. Over the next hour, another dozen families were represented, and she found her eyes following each of them the same way.

In a different world, that would have been her life. A house filled with shouting, laughter, skinned knees. A home. *Not my life*, she thought, twisting her neck to look up the street, stoutly ignoring the dry stinging of her eyes.

From inside the house, her phone rang just as she heard the motorcycle again, and she was up and headed indoors when she realized the rumble was loud, much louder than before. Booming to the point she wouldn't be surprised if all her neighbors came charging out to see what was happening, hands protectively over their ears, turned-down mouths mutely protesting against the intrusive flood.

Echoing from the houses across the way, the direction the sound was emitting from wasn't clear until she saw a long, double line of motorcycles round the corner, turning up her street. Frozen in place, she watched as the riders passed her, their eyes moving neither left nor right.

Then, near the end, exactly at the back of the line, she saw someone she knew. Knew, but didn't know. Didn't know, but wanted to *know*. She saw him. *HIM*. When she did, the memory of that day in the grocery store hit her. The day she put herself out there only to get shot down so hard it was a wonder the crater from her fall wasn't visible from space.

She had rounded the end of the aisle and seen a man. Tall, broad shouldered, he'd worn his jeans and thermal like a second skin. Full head of dark, thick hair. Strong, muscular. Gripping her basket by the handles, she'd walked close enough to catch a hint of his scent. So exactly what she would have expected, nothing except musk and man. Then he'd dropped a box and, not sure if it was intentional, she'd decided she would not pass up the chance to talk to him.

It wasn't until she'd retrieved the box and was straightening that she looked at his face and saw the scarring. Dark red and tight, the raised and painful looking grafts ran along the hinge of his jaw, the result of treatments for deep burns. The pocked surface of his cheeks, nose, and forehead held deep hollows from trauma, surrounded by alternating rough and smooth skin. Full lips firmly pressed into a thin line. Then he'd looked at her, and all she'd seen were his eyes.

Deep brown, intense, expressive, warm, and outrageously gorgeous. His personality, his being, shone from those eyes, and at that moment, the scarred face became unimportant. She saw the man, liked what she saw, and wanted him to know it. She issued a teasing dare, thrilled when he took her up on it, and then his lips were on hers. Chastely executed, her belly had still clenched when he'd leaned in, and she'd felt the heat from his mouth. Firm, controlled, his head had tilted the slightest, rightest amount.

If he had held the kiss a nanosecond longer, she would have entirely embarrassed herself by swiping his delicious bottom lip with the tip of her tongue. But he hadn't, and neither had she. He had pulled back, staring down at her and she'd watched how his eyes widened, flaring with what she hoped was arousal, attraction. She'd waited for a beat, then another, carving out a final stuttering second, holding her ground against the urge to flee in the face of what felt like a rebuff.

She pinpointed the moment she'd known it was rejection as the emotion in his gaze shut down, causing her hope to collapse in on itself, feet forced to step backwards a stride into the blackhole of dismissal, then another. With offhand words, she'd withdrawn, fleeing up the aisle, turning at the last moment to see him still staring at her. No reaction to the kiss, and no response to her final good-bye, the lamest flick of her fingers possible.

Then he was out of sight, and she had run to the checkout, dropping her basket onto the belt. Carelessly dumping the few items gathered before the encounter, she'd stared at them as they'd rolled around, the jerking movement carrying them to the cashier's hands to then be placed into a bag. She'd paid without looking at the boy running the register, convinced the embarrassment of what happened was written on her face in the blazing blood under her skin, branded by the rejection.

Now here the man was, riding a motorcycle down the street in front of her house. No doubt it was the same man. Strong, virile, he'd shown her with a single kiss that the fumbling boys of her past never had a chance. She heard his voice in her head, two words lifting her on a wave of hope and anticipation, *A kiss*.

Tilting her head, she twisted to look up the street, watching as the lines of motorcycles disappeared under the canopy of leaves.

How's the head?

Threading her fingers together, she levered the twined digits against her belly. A futile attempt to hold in anxious fears as she mentally compared the voices. Rational thought fled, squeezing through the physical strainer, skin and bone no barrier to awareness.

Taking that to mean she connected.

Rough and filled with humor, the tone clear in her head. Boldness mixed with desire. *A kiss.*

Her hallway lurker's identity was positively confirmed. He was the scarred man from the grocery store. Her humbling hero.

BRUTE

Motherfucking asshole, Brute thought as the club rolled through the residential streets. *Gunny did this just to fuck with me. I shoulda peeled off soon as I realized where he was leading us.*

As they'd walked out of the clubhouse this morning, Gunny had slung an arm around his neck, bringing Brute close to blow a loud raspberry against the side of his head. Crowing as he released Brute, Gunny told everyone around that today would be Brute's lucky day. With an exaggerated wink, Gunny had sauntered to his classic knucklehead, cheers and jeers sounding when his attempts to kick the thing to life succeeded on only the fifth or sixth attempt.

Riding in his position at the end of the columns, Brute played nursemaid for the day. Tailgunner for the run, his job to ensure no one was left behind. Wrench-wreck breakdowns, fuel fools, bladder busters—they were all his responsibility on this ride, and he took the charge seriously. So seriously he didn't heed the corners taking them out of their way, bringing a cloud of fuel and grease and noise to the sweet and quiet street that ran in front of a cottage he knew well. Turns long memorized flew past in a flash as he followed his brothers.

The last twist of the throttle, pushing left and then cocking back, feet to his highway bars as he rode straight towards her house in broad daylight. *Let it be my lucky day*, he prayed, knowing from the sun on his skin it would not be. Knowing from the strolling sentinels stalking the sidewalks that his girl would be perched on her plot, contemplating the entities surrounding her. She'd be wedged on her box, watching the ebb and flow of humanity walking past her door.

From half a block away, he saw her. How could he not? She was that brilliant, a precious gem flashing in the sunshine. Frozen in place, hand on the door, she had turned to face the noise of the bikes, and he angled his eyes to drink her in. Hip-hugging shorts, barely covering the enticing swell of her ass, longer than long legs tucked into short socks, the curves in between beauty incarnate. Breasts filling out the front of her short-sleeved tee, V-neck dipping low, promised treasures he had seen and chastely touched, never tasted. Wanted to taste. *God*, wanted so much more.

Flashing past, he imagined her head turned to look at him, tracking him down the street. Recognizing him. Dreamed in broad daylight that she knew him. Wanted him. A delayed look in his mirror proved that false, her escape into the cottage complete, leaving him exactly where he had always been. Outside looking in through the careful barrier that held their worlds separate. His view distorted like the night in the bar, beveled edges of the peephole bending light. *I'll hold onto my dreams for a while longer*, he thought, lifting his gaze to the row after row of bikes in front of him. *My girl, my dream*.

For now, he put all thoughts of Bexley aside. Even dialed back the rolling anger at his brother, because luck hadn't been with him.

Attention focused on the men in front of him, Brute reacted instinctively when the palm down signal traveled the column well before the crimson glow of brake lights flashed from the tails of the two dozen bikes. A left turn was indicated, and he slowed, slipping easily onto the end of the dragon's mechanical tail whipping one bike wide as they flowed through the corner and onto the main street.

Five minutes later, they merged into traffic on the highway and headed south, rolling downstate for a meet with another club, hoping to come to an understanding of boundaries. Today should help them draw unfuzzied lines to sharply demark where passage was allowed, and where forbidden.

Brute settled into his position in the rear, sliding effortlessly from side to side as needed so he could keep watch on his brothers. Nearer to the city, his job became more hectic, pulling into play dangerous skills hard learned. Swinging wide to force a car away, brushing close to a bumper to push back a cage threatening to cut the column.

Other tailgunners might use more permanent or showy methods of crowd control in traffic, leaving fear ricocheting like the sonic boom of their get-back whip sounding against a citizen's windshield. They might enjoy the satisfaction of seeing a steam-spewing cage limp to the shoulder, radiator plugged with nuts or bearings, no longer swarming the bikers rolling on their merry way. Brute's weapon of choice: his face. The mask besting every comer, lead-footed drivers instinctively giving terrified way to the hideous monster on the motorcycle.

Later on the run, his job changed again, as the column rolled deep in the city, down surface streets past rotting warehouses, empty of everything except squalid human remains. Decaying from the inside as they stared blankly at broken walls, submerged in the paralyzing amnesia of their choices. Here he was sentry against blind ambush. Watching. Gaze in perpetual motion, scanning and cataloging their surroundings, plotting differing lines of escape with every block deeper they rode into enemy territory.

Ahead lay the rival's clubhouse and false safety. Gate opened wide an innocent invitation, small pools of available parking inconveniently split, requiring their men to halt on either side of the structure. A vast expanse of openness between their forces was a potential killing field of black asphalt. Doorway approach was blocked by bikes; kickstands propped with front wheels angled, pegs down; they impeded escape from the building like wire-wrapped crosses on a beach.

Brute dismounted from his bike, swinging his leg in a smooth movement off and over to stand motionless but for his eyes. As Gunny approached, the remembered anger of betrayal swarmed him, climbing his insides in blistering stripes of rage. One of few able to read Brute's scarred and impassive mien, Gunny halted his advance, leaving a buffer of fifteen feet. Just enough. Barely enough.

"Good call, *brother*." Brute finally acknowledged his own anger, rising pressure in his jaw where the posts of implants were buried deep in the bone. He knew the muscles in his jaw and neck would be twisting the ridges of his skin. "Stopping out of reach." He paused and drew breath through his nose, blowing it out through barely parted lips. The movement caused memories to stir of wearing a mask in truth. Some days it had seemed the tiny, round holes in the rigid plastic barely allowed room for air. "Not the time or the place, but I will say this…" Shaking his head, he selected his words with care. "Of everyone… you know. Know what she means to me. You just didn't fucking care, did you?"

"*Brother*." Gunny's dismay was real, ringing true through his voice, his pained eyes. Heart-felt consternation at the weeping wounds and devastation his actions wrought. "I didn't think."

"No, you just *did*." Brute sucked in another breath, trying frantically to keep a grip on the control slipping through his fingers like ice in a red-hot skillet, wildly hurtling towards ruin. He gave an inch to his need for this man to understand, someone he called friend in addition to brother, and inclined forward, leather cut moving on his shoulders with the bunching of muscles. "*She saw me.*"

Brute stood upright, dragging the reins of his anger with him, readying himself to lay it down for now. The club required it.

Slate was striding towards them; their president's face a different kind of mask. Brute had learned each member held their own privately splintered expressions. One their own, the person they showed family and friends. And one for the club.

The club sustained Brute, made him a man again. Worthy and good, the club needed differences set aside in moments like these. On the enemy's ground, his focus had to be the advantage of the whole, not an avoidable altercation. To do otherwise was a betrayal of its own, something he could never tolerate.

"We got business, brother." He crossed to Gunny, pacing out the five strides that separated them on this lot. The look on Gunny's face said it all; he was steeling himself for pain that wasn't mental. Steeling himself to take with honor the answer his actions had earned. And he would, without complaint. He would stomach what Brute felt was needed to even the tottering balance held guaranteed by the patch riding their backs.

Seeing the willingness of his brother to accept whatever Brute needed to get past this moment gave him pause. *Not deliberate then, a true miscalculation.* Lifting a hand, he clasped Gunny's shoulder, stress sliding out of his brother at the firm hold, relief rushing in to fill the void. Brute asked, "We good?" He would leave acceptance of the fix in his brother's hands, maintaining friendships took effort from both sides. Maintaining brotherhood requiring more.

"We're good." Gunny's breath gusted out, and he grunted as Slate's footsteps reached them, drawing them both back to action.

BRUTE

He backed into his space, not a garage. They weren't available at his apartment complex, but he paid for an awning space. Since he rode year-round, he felt it worth the cost. He paid for privacy, too. Living behind a gate might bother some of his brothers, but for Brute, it gave him a peace of mind needed to breathe easy. A guard post against infiltrators. Visitors were required to check in, and even the simple sign-in sheet logging meant most things could be known if needed. The routine had become so comfortable over the past year, he sometimes didn't even look at the spaces up front, wouldn't know if there were new tenants until he saw them in passing.

Sometimes Brute wondered if the apartment manager warned new renters about him. "Oh, yeah. Almost forgot to mention it. About the guy in building twenty-one, apartment C. Just steer clear and you won't have anything to worry about. He's fine, not a danger, don't worry about that. It's just...the war. He was in the war, you know." That way when the new folks caught sight of him, they wouldn't warp as far sideways as they might otherwise, his face still a shock but buffered. The words would be an investment on the apartment complex's part, ensuring full disclosure. Reminiscent in a way of how realtors had to do if there was a murder in a house. This time, the death had only been a man's dreams. A face, but not a life.

It was nearly a month after they had ridden to Indy. Almost a month of Gunny working to repair a brotherhood that Brute had already decided wasn't damaged. The bastard was bending over backwards to work it out, though, and that shit was fun to see. He'd cut his brother some slack soon, rub him wrong in a way that let Gunny know Brute was so far past the event it didn't shade his rearview.

The previous weeks had seen some oddities, but between work and the club, Slate and the Rebels had kept him so busy he hadn't found time to focus on his girl as much as he liked. Since he'd walked out of her house, she'd kept her head down for the most part, working and then heading home alone, or going to her brother's to hang. The two times she had gone out had been back to the bar in New Haven, which was fucked up, because there were a lot of places closer to hand that held a better clientele, people more in her social circles. But, she returned to the dive.

Brute had been busy both times. Out on a run, he'd only been alerted when the dishwasher at the bar texted to let him know she'd showed. That was their deal—the boy texted, Brute paid. And he was happy to pay the kid. Glad he'd thought to set the arrangement up, especially when his instincts were right, and she wouldn't let what happened put her off the place.

One of his brothers dispatched to the bar because Brute deemed the mission too critical for prospect assignment, that brother asked to find a place close but not too close. Told to keep her safe. A careful distance requiring mature and focused judgment. Chafed at him, sending someone out like that, because it was "My job," he muttered, lifting his leg and swinging it off the bike.

Bending to the saddlebags, he pulled out the few groceries he had stowed. The shelves in his small pantry were nearly empty, which meant he really needed to take his truck to the store soon, stock up so he didn't have to fuck around with bare handfuls of shit at a time. Each time he braved the store was a chance for someone's reaction to start eating at him, so his preference was to reduce the opportunities for that public exposure. Fuck, if the store delivered, he'd keep them in business singlehandedly.

He buckled and locked the bag, then straightened, turning to walk under the stairs to his door. There was a shadowy figure standing there. Locking down his first instinct to rush in and confront or subdue whoever it was, he stood still, waiting. If the person, woman by the shape and size, would only take a step into the light, he would know friend or foe. Movement, at first hesitant and slow, disclosed curves instead of angles. Definitely a woman.

"Ricky?" Such a soft voice, unsure of her welcome, but at least one he knew.

He broke free from the caution holding him in place, anger rushing to fill the void caused by adrenaline, followed quickly by a drowning fear. "Natalie? What the fuck, Natty?" Daughter of his best friend from childhood, his goddaughter, that honor granted before his first deployment. Overseas, heat and exhaustion and hunger in the field had been cut through with each delivery of emailed snapshots and vids. Him a distant witness to her first step, first word, first grade, first date.

Back before the war took everything else from him.

When recovery was assured, but his condition was not, mired in impotent anger and depression he had contacted Dylan from the hospital, tried to beg off. He'd told him to find someone more suited to a girl who at that time was barely a teen and into boys, her beauty calling for things from him that he couldn't find within himself to give.

Dylan had rocked his world, telling him what Natty had needed wasn't something the blast stripped from him. In his injury, Dylan said that he could give her a lesson few learned. She didn't need to be shown that imperfect things could be cast aside, but that they became more precious in their imperfection. Brute hadn't spoken in response, unable to, silent throat closed so tightly that even swallowing had become impossible. Choked breathing the only sound, their call had ended in quiet, broken finally by Dylan's solemn promise, "We'll see you soon, brother."

Once back on US soil, a resolved Brute had appeared on their front porch. No warning, not wanting to ease into it, he provided no previsit explanation of what had happened to him. And his friend had demonstrated the truth of what Brute had known since they were seven and pledged themselves as blood brothers, that oath costing him five stitches when the dull blade had slipped, slicing his finger all to hell and back. Clenching hands slippery with blood, the promise had soaked into his soul much like the crimson liquid soaked into the dirt floor of the barn.

Blindly trusting his gut, Brute had arrived on the doorstep of a man who held beautiful in his hands every day. A man who stood in his shoes without ever having known anything other than goodness and light in his life. Dylan's wife and daughter were so gorgeous a man would cross the street for a chance to walk in their shadow. And, proving that long ago pain worth the bearing, that man hadn't reacted beyond the first involuntary flinch, and even at the moment, Brute knew Dylan's recoil was pain for what Brute had suffered, not because his friend's stomach was rolling with nausea at what he saw.

Then Dylan's wife had shown beyond a doubt she was worth every minute of the man's care and love of her. She had she met Brute with the same, reaching up to press her hand flat against the hard plastic mask he wore in those days, letting the heat seep into his face through the barrier against touch. Her only question proof that she could stand firm in whatever storm might come her way, "Beer or whiskey?"

Before Brute could answer, Natalie had surged headlong down the stairs at her father's call of, "Natty, Pappa Ricky's here." Fabric-covered feet soundless on the steps, the swell of her voice his radar track pointing to her advancement through the house. Excited and already jabbering a mile a minute when she turned the corner from the hallway into the kitchen, she hadn't even hesitated in her headlong approach before throwing herself into his embrace.

Wrapping her thin girl's arms around his chest, she held on tightly, mouth still going, chattering about everything of importance that had crossed her mind since they'd last spoken. Safe in his arms, cheek pressed against his chest. When she finally tipped her head up, words turning to a question at his lack of response, looking into his face for the first time sent her silent.

He had stood, waiting for the horror to hit as her intense gaze tracked across his features. Waited for the wails and wet-tracked cheeks, waited for the shoulder shove to escape revulsion's embrace. Motionless, shuddering in anticipation, he waited, knowing what she saw and already not blaming her.

His lashless eyes staring, bulging at her from a raw and ruined face, looking too large for their sockets from the way the scars and grafts pulled at his skin. Lips red and puffy, pushing through the hole in the mask, the flesh all around compressed, held in place. Scars and angry mottled skin grafts visible through the hard plastic, color ranging from maroon to pale gray. One ear burned down to nothing, a stub where it used to be.

"Hey," she'd told him softly, giving him a squeeze. "God, I love your eyes. My Pappa Ricky."

And, just as easy as that, the new him, the damaged thing left behind in the wake of the blast, found a way to fit into their lives. Not the same, but different in a manner that suited the present. And now, Natty was here, a thousand miles away from where she was supposed to be, looking anxious and afraid.

"What's wrong, Natty?" He called the question but was already on the move, crossing the space between them, bending down to look into her face as he transferred things to one hand. He stared as he pulled the keys from his pocket. She'd been crying, recently and a lot, if the swollen lids told the truth. "What's wrong?" His repeated question garnered no response. It looked like she was so lost in her head he wasn't even sure if she was hearing him.

She stood there, gazing up at him and he watched while the weight of what she was carrying broke her, her face shifting from only just holding it together to totally lost, capsizing in the space of a single breath. The corners of her mouth turned down, and her chin was quivering as it had when she was seven, and her cat escaped their house, but couldn't outrun the traffic on a nearby street. Brute had been there that evening, had gone out with a shovel and bag to bring the remains home. Had stood in the backyard as Natty sat crumpled on the grass beside a shoebox-sized patch of bare dirt, sobbing. Had crouched next to her, gathering the girl she was then into his lap, settling them on the ground while she showed him the burden of grief and loss she'd felt.

Standing in front of him now, she squeezed her eyes shut, turning her head away, neck twisting to pull her chin to her shoulder. Bracing for a blow, she expected whatever this was to upset him, and feared his reaction. Keys in hand, he reached out, tugging her close, taking the hit as she buried her face in his chest. That was when the tears started, and he turned them together towards his door, needing to get the wailing child out of the apartments' shared breezeway.

"Work with me, Nat," he muttered, shoving the key into the lock and twisting, then pushing the door with his foot. He dropped the groceries to the floor just inside the entrance, then maneuvered her towards the couch. "Couple more feet, hon." Brute sat, and Natty did what she'd always done when he was close, ever since she was old enough to crawl, and that was climb into his lap like a kitten. She snuggled in, nestling into his hold, secure in the knowledge that he would never turn her away, never hurt her, never make her feel less than protected. He was her safe port in any storm, always would be.

"Give it to me, honey. Give it all to me," Brute crooned into Natty's ear, her body jolting with the force of her sobs. His hand soothed up and down her back, gently providing solid confirmation she was supported, was loved, wouldn't be left out there alone where her terror lay in wait. "Give it to me, baby girl. Give it. You can't hold all this, Natty girl, give it."

"It hurts, Pappa Ricky." That name from her, something she hadn't called him in years, nearly broke his control and his heart in one stroke. Her behavior, her reactions, every nuance of this visit had each fine hair lifting on his body, prickles of anticipated rage sweeping over him. A flash flood of fear.

"What hurts, baby girl? Give it to me." His persistent plea worked, or she had gotten to a place in her pain where she could turn it into words, passing it out like IOU cards at an early holiday party.

"I hurt," she amended her statement. Every muscle in his body seized when she continued, in a voice soft as velvet, as jagged as rotten ice in a mountain stream, all smooth and easy on the surface and broken-toothed danger underneath, "He hurt me."

***

Hearing her stumble through her pained recitation of events, he refused to leave even when the ER doctor flat ordered him. The doc's commanding presence and Aussie accent were not intimidating to Brute. He looked straight at the man and told him, "I ain't fucking leaving her alone."

A quick, shuttered glance at Natty gave the doc the same story; she didn't want Brute to go. Looked like she'd come unstuck if he did, face already gone white at the threat. He and the doc embarked on a two-minute stare down, broken only when a nurse came into the room. Without turning his head, the doc spoke a code number that sent the nurse scurrying.

Nearly three hours later, Brute held Natty upright with an arm around her waist as the nurse gave out final instructions. From the corner of his eye, Brute watched as the doc walked their way. He stopped in front of Brute and Natty, held out a hand, and when she tentatively reached out, he cradled hers between both of his. "You'll come good out of this, promise. She'll be apples in the end."

He turned to Brute and eyed him up and down, clinically assessing his injuries. "You've healed well, but you're ignoring the therapy, mate. Makes the scars mad as a cut snake. Whatever cream you're on to using now, stop. It's bodgy as hell." He released Natty's hand, dug in his back pants pocket for his wallet, and pulled out a card. "I got a practice. Come see me, right?"

Taking the card without saying a word, Brute had turned Natty towards the doors, intent on heading to his truck in the parking garage when the doctor spoke from behind him. "I see you lot in here often." Twisting his neck, Brute looked back at him. "I'm Bulldog." Brute stared at him because that didn't make sense. Why the fuck would this doc have a road name? "I served with bikies overseas. Fixed up my fair share." Bulldog smiled. "Some men you know. Gunny, while we were over there." Spoken with a head jerk, that got Brute's full attention because this was a solid connection worth exploring. Bulldog continued, drawing the circle nearly closed. "And Bear, over here." Brute turned more fully, Natty sagging against him as they shifted back to face the doc. "Delivered your man's boy not long ago."

What the hell? The thought ran through Brute's mind, and he knew he was gaping now.

"His blood's worth bottling, that Mason. He's a good'un, liked what I've seen of him. Heaps." Bulldog pointed at the card Brute still held, loosely gripped in his fingers. "I'm only on the helping side, here. You're right to be holding back, but you can use friends, I reckon. We all can, yeah?" Bulldog took a step backwards, making a shooing motion with one hand. "Take your girlie home, it'll come good. We'll see ya." He tipped his head in farewell and Brute found himself returning the gesture.

Home and settled, he got Natty to bed, hoping the pills would help her doze while he took care of business. He would ease things for her, make it better so she didn't have to break the news, just reassure the ones who loved her that she'd be okay. He tapped a corner of his phone against his forehead a moment, using the shocks of pain to center his thoughts before dialing to deliver news no parent should ever hear.

"No, brother, I don't know why she didn't come home." This was to Dylan, part of the three-way call Brute was on, the other participant being Dylan's wife. "Doc said she's okay physically. They did all the bloodwork needed, talked her through what she needs to watch for." Standing in the hallway, he sucked in a breath, staring through the door at the blanket-bundled form on his guest bed.

"I've got a couple of friends who've been through this," he said, and he did, the little band of Rebels in the Fort had gathered their fair share of people damaged by the world, including two women he knew who had been raped. He'd already placed a call to Slate's old lady, Ruby, setting up an introduction for the morning. Ruby would take one look at Natty and shift directly into protective mother-hen mode. And he knew, once she had this chick under her wing, it wouldn't be an hour before their girl had a huddle of women with her, every one of them good as gold and ready to throw down on her behalf. "She's gonna talk to one of them tomorrow. Then see a counselor in the afternoon."

He drew breath in, deep and slow, because next up was talking around the edges of the dangerous bits. He knew what he was going to do, had already started the process by placing that call, too. If Natty was his little girl by blood, not just—*what a farce, she could never be "just" anything to me*—his goddaughter, he would be raging at the news. He was raging, just inside, holding it together so Dylan could vent his out, as he had before getting Natty's mother on the phone, promising retribution to the stupid-as-fuck man who had violated their little girl.

What Brute planned to do wasn't something he could talk about, because he'd involved his brothers. No way would he risk them feeling any blowback from this. *My shit won't seep*, he promised himself, and then shared part of the truth with Dylan. "She doesn't know the guy's name." At least it wasn't someone she trusted—a small solace sure, but something.

"Only saw his face in shadow." Meant she couldn't identify him to the cops who came to the ER, but Brute had picked away at what she did know until he thought there was enough.

"Cops got what they could, which wasn't much." Not a lie, but Dylan didn't need to know he gleaned much more of a harvest than the boys in blue. "She's afraid, now. Scared out of her mind. Scared she'll see him."

The small campus she attended wasn't hard to navigate, but deafening dread thundered in her head. From her words, he knew it tore at her thoughts that her attacker could be anyone. In her mind, he became everyone. Was in every place. The possibility of turning any corner to find him there was what drove her to her car. Even away from campus, she couldn't shake the fear. As Brute had listened, she'd talked a bit about her trip. Miles and miles rolling under her wheels, each set of headlights to hit her rearview intimidating. He could see how that possibility had pierced her, and with tissues clutched in her fingers, even cradled safely in his lap she still wept as she talked about it.

"Dylan. Man." A breath. "Brother, she wants to stay here for a bit." He eased this out, waiting for the shouted denial but Dylan surprised him.

"We'll call the school, see what we can do to get her classes taken care of." Silence for a moment, then a soft, "You're gonna go careful, yeah?"

"Yes." He made this single word as solid and confident as he could, envisioning a wall of bricks holding back the world from his girl. "She's safe with me, Dylan."

"She should have been safe at school," his friend's voice was rough, ragged, and Brute could envision the man standing across the room from his wife, tore up about what happened, but holding it together for her and Natty.

"Shoulda. Wasn't," Brute said slowly, making sure Dylan heard him. Heard what he couldn't say. "She is here."

Call over, the disconnect severed the threads that held Brute to be reasonable. He thumbed his phone again, eyes never leaving the unmoving blankets. What he saw was different. He saw, as if they were still there, the scene from inside the exam room in the ER.

Natty lay on her back on a narrow bed, head turned so she could keep Brute in view. Minute twitches of muscle in her face and neck hinted at her discomfort as the doc worked, murmuring to the nurse about this thing or that procedure.

Natty's hands fisted in the thin gown at her sides, he'd already seen the half-moon craters gouged in her palms from before. A metallic click sounded, and a second later, she jumped in place. Her face scrunched up, tears welling in her eyes at what the man at the foot of the table was doing. A moment later it was over, and the doc stood from the stool, avoiding the sheet spread on the floor, and gently patted her leg. "I'm going to step out, Natalie.

The nurse will just be a moment more." His voice was compassionate when he said, "We need to get photos." He cut his gaze to Brute, then back to the girl on the table. "I'll be back in a few minutes."

A tear broke free, trailing across the bridge of her nose and down her cheek, then another. Brute reached out, cupping her face in his hands, gaze locked with hers. Willing her to be strong, to be okay, to get through this. More tears flowed, and he swept them from her face with his thumbs. "Natty." He heard his own voice, unrecognizable with the cargo of anguish it carried.

"We're on it, brother." Gunny's voice shook him free of the memories.

"Need you to come to me." This would be hard for Gunny to see, hard for him to hear, with his woman's history. She was the other one Brute knew who had survived years of abuse. He needed Gunny here, wanted to know how to handle someone you loved when this happened. The relationship might be different, but he figured people were the same.

"On my way." That was all he had got before the call ended, cutting off all background noise. He thumbed the phone again, looking down at the device as he did so. A moment later, he had another voice, this one from farther west, his gateway to whoever this marked fucker was.

"Chief," he began, and then got a surprise because he expected to have to introduce himself, but that was not the case. Without uttering another word, he got what he needed.

"Brute. Already got the call, friend." The voice reflected the owner, steady and confident. Chief was president of a Utah club, friendly with the Rebels, and the closest to where Natty had been attending college. "We got a description, but I'm glad you called. I have a couple of questions. Got the time?"

For Natty, he'd make the time, always. "Yeah," he answered, then waited.

"Day and time, that'll help narrow down who was there and who wasn't. We have a couple of connections down Salt Lake way, headed them up towards Ogden already." Ogden was the campus location. "They're in the wind, but I want to have everything we can when they check in next. Walk me through it. Make me see it, Brute. Don't hold back, the smallest thing can be the key."

Chief had been FBI once, a lifetime ago, and while he had lost faith in the government who'd employed him, he had not lost the skills. Brute spent the next twenty minutes talking, feet pacing a path through his kitchen to the patio, back to the kitchen. Voice low, not wanting Natty to hear, he worked through everything he knew, which was a fuckton more than the cops did. The blues who showed up to the ER didn't listen, didn't hear, even when things were laid out, because they weren't empowered the way an outlaw was. Their hearing was honed to pitches that lined up with their capabilities.

Brute heard the wind bending around the corner, saw the chances not taken.

A bike in the lot roared and cut off, engine dying as he disconnected that call on promises of frequent updates. He beat Gunny to the door, opening and leaving it swinging behind him. A quick glance showed Natty still asleep, granted the surcease of peace for a time, at least.

***

"You need to absent yourself, Brute." Speaking softly, Ruby stared straight into his face. The tiny redhead wasn't afraid of anyone, and proved it often, as she did now. "Natalie and I will be all right." As Ruby said this, she turned her head, smiling at the girl seated on the couch beside her. Natty's eyes didn't see the smile, didn't lift from where they focused on a point just past her knees. She had been like this most of the morning, withdrawn and quiet since getting off a tearful call with her parents. "In fact, I often go to the group session she's scheduled for." Twisting her head, she winked at Brute. "I'll just haul her happy butt along with me when I go today."

Abruptly standing, Ruby clapped her hands, the sound startling in the quiet apartment. Even that noise didn't capture Natty's attention, and Ruby grimaced. Hand on Brute's arm, she guided him to the kitchen. In a low voice, she said, "I get what she's doing. The talk with her folks this morning wore her down. Now she's trying to find space to recharge, but how she's doing that won't work. She can't find solace within, not right now. I know what she needs, Brute. Let me have her."

He was so tense her fingers could barely dent the skin of his biceps when she squeezed. "Trust me. Give me until after the group. Meet us there for her appointment. She'll have to talk then. I know from experience this doc doesn't let you slack off. That way you'll be right there with her, ready to be her rock when someone expects the hardest things out of her. She can lean on you then, and you can do what's needed. For the group, she can just observe. Stay totally quiet, unless she doesn't want to be. But she needs to hear that there is healing after this kind of pain."

He stared at her for a minute, and she held his gaze. Steady and patient, just like she was with her kids. With two sets of twins, the oldest entering their toddling years, patience wasn't just a virtue, it was a necessity. "She matters to me, Ruby."

"I know she does, honey. I can see that." She reassured him, the words coming immediately on the heels of his statement. "She's not fine right now, not in her head as she is, but she'll be fine with me." Serious eyes held his gaze. Ruby had never lied to him, and he didn't expect she'd begin now, with something this important. Hesitantly, he nodded, and she squeezed his arm again. "We'll get her through this, Brute."

Four hours later, he drove onto the parking lot for the clinic, angling the truck into a spot near the doors. He didn't know how sore Natty still would be, three days later, but anything he could do to alleviate an ounce of it would be counted worth the effort. He checked his watch; five minutes until his appointment with Bulldog.

Her counselor and the doc were in the same building, and that seemed too big a coincidence to ignore, so he'd made a call earlier in the day, lucky enough to set up something the same time as her group.

He unfolded out of the truck, scanning the lot out of habit as he walked. A blonde head moving through the vehicles plucked at his attention, the too-familiar color and height of the woman ringing alarm bells. She was walking towards the building, too, making her way between the parked cars and trucks, weaving back and forth so it was at least another half a minute before he got a clear look at her face. When he did, his feet stopped moving, and he dropped his head immediately, tracking her still, but doing it without looking directly at her. *Fuck*. Bexley.

A half a second from retracing his steps in escape, he heard someone call her name at the same time Natty called his. *Fuck*. Lifting his head, he saw Natty and Ruby, arm-in-arm beside the doors, Natty looking in his direction and Ruby looking across the lot. *Fuck*. Raising his hand, he turned his back to Bexley, shouting across to Natty, "Forgot something. See you after, yeah?" Jogging back to his truck, he folded into it, shoved the keys into the slot and twisted them, hearing the engine roar.

When he looked up, the small cement landing in front of the doors was empty, and a scan of the lot showed no blonde heads, familiar or not. Only a few people, all women, scurrying towards the doors as if they were afraid to be seen. Shame camouflaged as urgency, tense muscles an internal protest line the women crossed each time they entered the building.

On his phone, recent calls gave him easy access to the doc's service, where he called to let them know he'd be a few minutes late. Then he sat in the truck until well after the group session was to begin, then waited for another five, just for good measure. The entire time his mind raced, trying to make sense of what had just happened. The look of the women walking in after Natty and Ruby, he had to think they were all there for the same thing. Counseling. But not just any kind of talking doc, this was rape counseling. The idea of what Natty endured enraged him, her body used in a way that took what should be a beautiful act bringing two people together and trashed the idea of intimacy.

He knew Ruby's story, and at the thought, the rage was there, too. She had been trapped in a windowless room for months, president of a rival club using her as the mood struck him. The only thing that kept any of the brothers sane was knowing that man was no longer sucking her air. Natty's attacker was upright and breathing. "Not for long," he muttered, heading up the stairs to the second floor where Bulldog's offices were, even the knowledge that they were close to picking up the bastard scarcely soothing him.

Bexley. *She's here, in this building*, he thought, following the hallway, feet and legs moving by rote. The memory of her body, soft and rounded. Beautiful. Vulnerable. Dusky rose peaks on her breasts, the way her legs folded into her body, her scent. A treasure he treated with care. Would always handle with care, if entrusted with that precious duty. Something, if he was reading the signs right, that suffered unspeakable abuse, an intruder forcing their way. Fury rose within him, swift and fierce, blood pounding through his veins, in his head, demanding he find who had done that to, "*My girl*."

He leaned his forearms against the wall just outside Bulldog's office, fighting for control of the anger seething in him, that rage feeling like a living thing, writhing just underneath the skin. The door opened abruptly, and he jerked back, staggering against the opposite wall, staring down at the doc. Without acknowledging the struggle Brute knew had to be screaming from his face, Bulldog turned his back, leaving the door standing wide, calling over his shoulder, "Come on in, grab a cup, head to the back." He stepped behind the receptionist desk, shuffling through papers as Brute hesitated in the doorway. Without looking up, Bulldog told him, "Close it behind ya. No need to let the world in."

An hour later, Brute stood back in the same place, paused a half step over the threshold listening to Bulldog call to him, "Next week, back here same as we did, right?" Unsure what he actually agreed to, he nodded, taking the next half step to the hallway, shutting the door behind him. Experimentally, he opened his mouth wide, jaw muscles cracking with disuse, feeling the skin on his cheeks and neck wrench and pull, stinging with the movement but not hurting. There was no searing pain as he would usually experience, the ultrasound and massage utilized by Bulldog alleviating his discomfort by no small margin over what it had been before.

The entire elevator ride down to street level, he continued to push and test the boundaries of his new-found reprieve, stopping short of the movements that stretched bound-in rigidity too far but enjoying the breadth of the newly-discovered comfort zone. Encouraged for the first time in the eternity that had seemed his life, he felt the bounce and sway of the elevator car as it reached the floor, leveling with the surface before the doors opened wide. Distracted, he was two strides into the lobby before the gaggle of women standing around registered and by that time escape was impossible, the doors pinging quietly behind him as they cut off retreat.

Gasps came from every side but he heard a ringing "Pappa Ricky," from ahead, so, he dipped his head to the side and turned towards the one voice he wanted to hear, knowing his Natty was at the end of the sound trail. Chin angled, he kept his face pointed towards the wall, edging the outside circumference of the group, hearing her tentative chatter dipping and waning. She wasn't sure about the situation or her audience, but like his Natty always did, she was trying hard to push through. "…meet my godfather, Ricky Monte."

Her feet in view now, he glanced up and froze. *How did I not see this as a possibility?*

Brute's beautiful girl, his gorgeous Bexley, stared up at him, gaze fixed on his *face*.

BEXLEY

My hero. That was the first thought to crash through her head. From her position in front and slightly to the side, she held his gaze as he rocked to a halt. She was vaguely aware of Natalie's introduction, hearing his name. But at seeing his face, *his eyes*, words flew from her head as she waited for a sign from him that he remembered her. That he was *real*. In the weeks since she'd seen him riding his iron mount down her street, she had nearly convinced herself that the grocery aisle kissing bandit had been as much a mental anomaly as her hallway lurker, neither real in the sense of her world. Her brain's way of protecting her against the ghosts these counseling sessions stirred.

Why she would imagine a man like hers, she had no idea. A cruel trick of her brain to conjure up one like this, able to command surrender with the slightest pressure of his lips against hers. What possible healing could she give herself by causing even more pain? Was it her own mind actively rejecting her damaged, meager charms?

My hero. Pounding fast, her heart demanded the illusion and her brain acquiesced, even going so far as to feed his scent into her flawed fantasy. Musk and man, just as she remembered.

As from a distance, she heard Ruby talking. They'd connected weeks ago after a particularly trying group session, one in which Bex had admitted to resorting to danger-seeking activities resulting in her being naked in bed. One in which she did not mention her hallway lurker.

Over the course of that single hour, Ruby had determined Bex needed someone in her life. The woman had proven herself a tenacious supporter, committed to dragging Bex kicking and screaming into a friendship. A ballast Bexley could use to keep the dangerous impulses at bay. Not five minutes after the session was over, Ruby was tucking her phone away, Bex's number safely entered into the contacts, electronic storage of an association unfounded at the time. Since then the connections came, not every day, not even every other day, but regularly. At least twice a week Ruby's number came up on the screen in a call or a text. Just testing the waters, making sure things were steady, that the flow wasn't undermining Bex's resolve. Only twice had she ventured out, both times making it safe to home, no hallway lurker escort needed.

There was a pause in the background noise, a cessation of the conversation and Bex heard Ruby ask, "Brute, you okay, big guy?"

Ricky Monte, Natalie had called him, but Ruby's *Brute* seemed a far better fit.

Without looking away from his eyes, she felt his rumbling voice like a caress when he responded, "Yeah, Ruby." The timbre of his voice changed, adjusting to a lower register, resonating in all the right places when he continued, "I'm good."

It took a physical effort to move her gaze from his eyes, but she did it, proud of herself until she realized it hadn't gone far before becoming locked on his mouth instead. Sensuous lips. Lips she knew the shape and feel of, the heat and weight of, lips she wanted the right of entry to again, to confirm something she already knew. Eager admission that it had been the best kiss she'd ever had, it was a rare gift granted to her in a grocery store aisle.

A man of microscopic responses, she saw the upper line of his top lip change slightly, knew it was with pleasure but wasn't certain what had pleased him. Wanted to know so she could make sure it happened again, and again. Happened in a bigger way so he could be free to give her more, because she just knew that the more would be even better. Rich timbre still in effect, his lips parted, and he said her name, "Bexley."

Ball's in my court, she thought, running her tongue across her dust-dry lips, seeing another microscopic change. His lips moved, almost as if he were mirroring

68

her motion inside his closed mouth, lips proving a barrier to the tip of his tongue. Reflexively, she repeated the action and saw the same response. Liking his name, she liked the near-title Ruby bestowed on him better, and so she claimed that in a way she hoped he didn't miss. "Brute."

The inrush of breath at his name in her mouth surprised her, then she realized it was another of those microscopic tells she could see because she was so close. She didn't feel crowded, but he had kept coming towards where she stood with these two women who knew him. Kept moving until he was in her space, looking down, so close she could feel the heat from his body. So when he took a breath, she got to witness it, lips parting on a gasp, the wall of his chest expanding, his chin lifting slightly in a purely physical response.

Natalie spoke, and when she did, their shared moment was past. Brute's eyes closed in a blink, severing the connection and when his eyes opened again, his gaze was directed beyond her, pointed at Natalie. "Pappa Ricky? I need to head back to the doctor's office. But..." Her voice trailed off.

"I'm with you, Natty girl." Meant to be reassuring, but his rumble now was different from the last, a line of anger riding the sensation this time and Bex watched as his eyes flared, pupils expanding and then contracting at a memory or secret knowledge. "Right here, honey."

"I..." Natalie paused, then pushed through to what she and Ruby had been discussing just before Brute—*Brute*—walked off the elevator. "I want you there"—this came out in a rush, and the words following tumbled freefall from her lips, nearly running together as she fought to get them out—"but I need to talk to the doctor first. And I want Ruby with me when I do." Natalie's voice broke, exposing her fear. "Don't be mad, please don't be mad."

Proving he was plainly perfect, cementing the knowledge that he couldn't be real because men like him didn't exist, he immediately responded, "Never mad at you, baby girl. You can't upset me, honey. I'll give you what you need. You only gotta tell me like you did just now, and I'll break my back to give it to you."

He shifted slightly and Bexley watched as his arms lifted an inch, then two from his sides, presenting a hidden but open invitation she felt her body longing to accept; before she could move to claim something not hers, Natalie was there, and he wrapped her up tightly. So tight she didn't know how Natalie could continue breathing in air, but it must have been the right amount because the girl said softly, her voice gentle, not wheezing, "Love you, Pappa Ricky."

"Love you, too, Natty girl." Bex'd lost sight of his eyes. They were closed now, not squeezed shut with pain, but simply closed, blocking out stimuli so he could focus on the girl in his arms, making sure he gave her what she needed. Protecting. Holding on. Keeping her safe. A sheltered harbor for this girl so ill-used. "Let's get you back to the doc." Giving.

Without thought, Bex's mouth moved, tongue and lips giving voice to words she didn't expect. "I'll keep you company until they need you." That gained her his eyes again, lids flying open, intense whiskey-brown gaze directed her way, caution written there. He wasn't saying no but was wary of her for some reason. Maybe there were memories of her after all.

Natalie turned in his arms, fingers wrapping around his wrist as she stepped away from him, pulling out of the embrace in a way that looked like she'd been doing this since she was born. "That would be awesome, Bex."

The rumble moved through her again, and she shivered when he spoke. "Not necessary." He paused after this rejection, not the first she'd received from him. The pain she felt must have been visible because she got another eye flare and then he continued, voice carrying so much emotion the atmosphere around them became heavy, "But it would be welcome." He hesitated, then said, another odd intonation rushing through the rendition of her name, "Bex."

The next hour was a revelation because her Brute was real. Real and seated right beside her on an uncomfortable, plastic-covered couch that would otherwise have caused her to fidget and fuss, but today it didn't even register. She worked to get more of those responses, finding a thread he found humorous and tugging it gently, pulling and twitching it to milk more from him. They both carefully skirted the fact they knew the other, pretending for a non-existent public that this was their first encounter but knowing through their shared glances that the other thought about the stolen moments as they talked.

The only seeming misstep hers when, laughing quietly at something he said, she leaned close and rested her hand on his arm. Palm to his bicep, the touch so innocent if it hadn't been for the fact that the heat from his skin against her hand blazed through her, she wouldn't have paid it any mind, but he froze. At the touch, he locked into place, gaze focused with heated intensity on her face. He let her pull back, let her stammer out the first words of her request for forgiveness, embarrassed that she had broken the ease of their fitting together.

Using one of those microscopic movements, he shook himself, throwing off the moment and interrupting her feeble attempts at an apology by saying, "Liked it." Words locked in her throat, she waited, and he didn't disappoint, clarifying, "Liked you touching me, Bex." Then he blew her mind, approaching the events in their past that she, at least, had been skirting carefully. "Liked your kiss, too. Like everything about you, Bex. Too much, maybe."

She heard the squeak in her voice when she asked, "Too much?" She caught the eye flare again, his dark eyes warm on her and from the corner of her vision, she saw movement. She looked down to see his hand lifted a half an inch from where it had rested on his thick thigh, raised in her direction, as clear an invitation as his open arms had been to Natalie earlier. She accepted it just as quickly. Threading her hand through the air, she placed it in his, palm to palm, where warmth and heat that had nothing to do with body temperature and everything to do with arousal hit her. He cradled her hand, tugging slightly and lowering their joined grip until they rested on her thigh, the backs of his fingers scorching through her jeans.

His fingers tightened around hers as he answered, "Maybe…" He blinked, then continued, "Maybe just the right amount."

BRUTE

What in the fuck am I doing? Brute thought as he sat there on a day that should have been filled with nothing but shit, holding the hand of the woman he had watched for months, spoken with three times, and kissed for a barely-there moment. Her hand willingly placed in his, eagerly even, held on like it mattered to her. The reality of Brute's girl didn't disappoint. She was every bit as beautiful as he knew she was, but inside, where he still had bits of uncertainty before today, now existed clarity. The woman he thought her to be, proven beyond the shadow of a doubt.

After Natty had trailed the doctor into her office, head held bravely high, Ruby's hand in hers, Bexley perched on the edge of the couch's cushions. She hadn't said anything, just looked up at him expectantly, and he, not wanting to disappoint because he had seen the aftermath of that emotion on her face earlier, sat beside her. Those ticking moments after her impulsive offer to entertain him, an offer he had been about to decline until resignation flashed across her face, a hollow surety of rejection that tore at him. The joy that followed his acceptance was hard to miss and painted a layer of pleasure across his insides.

I made my girl happy, he thought, accompanying pleasure still echoing in his head while they talked, a give and take as sweet as candy. And just as addicting and something he wanted to hold onto forever. Then it happened. Her talking, him knowing where it was going and he finished one of her comments, their brains so in sync he knew what she'd been about to say, and in response, she'd laughed and touched him.

That touch caught him off guard, an unexpected boon as precious to him as the memory of her willing kiss. People who knew him weren't cautious with their approach, like Natty and Ruby. They knew he welcomed the chance to connect physically and reached across that chasm frequently. His girl, his Bex, how did she know he needed that? Then for her to take his reaction as dislike or distaste when it was so deeply the other direction, wounded him. So he gave her more, a solace for her jumbled nerves, firm reassurance that she hadn't crossed a line, that in fact, she had drawn one between them. Words, and she liked those, then his silent offer to extend that line and she had liked that even more. Attaching herself to him in a way that was unmistakable.

The door opened, doctor framed by the inner sanctum, beckoning him with a soft smile. Natty must be good, but this meant an end to their interlude. He turned to Bex and mouth open, prepared to say something. He didn't know what, but he wanted an offer to extend their time. She beat him to the punch, squeezing his hand tightly before telling him, "I'd like to see you."

With a nod, he stood, drawing her to her feet. A tug and she stumbled towards him, hand to his chest, chin tilted upwards. Looking into her eyes, he asked, "When?"

A glance over her shoulder and she looked back to him with a tiny frown, not much to see, but it was there. Cautious on Natty's behalf, she was weighing her wants and Natty's needs. "I think your schedule is the one we need to worry about." Confirmation that she wouldn't tread on someone else for her sole benefit. "I could cook if you wanted to bring Natalie for dinner." A statement, but the uplifting tone on the end turned it to a question, one written in her insecurities.

Leaning in, he told her, "I'll call you tonight," and damn him if she didn't sweep her bottom lip with the tip of her tongue, that action one that had caused his dick to jump in his jeans earlier, having the same effect on him now. "That okay?" Another sweep of her lip and he wanted to taste her mouth, that desire, need, deep inside him, boiling out in a heated flood.

She nodded and leaving her hand in his, reached back with her other. Palming her phone, she worked the buttons ineptly, but patiently, more disposed for this to take another moment longer than she was to release his hand. Eyes to his, she waited expectantly. Not willing to take the chance he'd give her a wrong number, she was ready to cement knowledge immediately. Numbers rolled, her thumb moved, his pocket gave a quiet ding, and she smiled. "Hold you to that," she murmured, pocketing her phone.

Across the room, a discretely cleared throat brought him back to the need at hand. "I gotta get in there for Natty." He told her something she already knew, and she smiled as she nodded. "I'll call you tonight," he reassured her, and the nods came double time, accenting her eagerness.

Ruby's voice came from the hallway, breaking the moment. "Bex, honey, I'll walk you out." Bexley released his hand as Ruby moved close, snugging an arm around his waist and giving him a sideways hug. "Brute, call me if Natty needs me. Anytime, honey. You call. Regardless, I'll be over tomorrow morning. I'll pick her up about eight. Some of the girls want to meet us for coffee."

Bexley lifted her head, eyes to Ruby as if weighing her words, balancing them against a probable rebuff, which seemed to be her go-to on things. A moment later Ruby had linked arms with her and, chatting, was guiding her up the hallway. The doctor had stepped into the waiting room, indicating the open doorway with one arm, and Brute walked from where he never expected to be, into a place he'd rather not know existed.

BEXLEY

Ruby didn't waste any time, and before they even cleared the front doors had asked, "So you and Brute? What you got going on there?"

Bexley looked at her, certain her confusion showed on her face. After a moment, she decided the safest route through this potential minefield was a redirection, so she asked, "How do you know him?"

Surprisingly, Ruby was immediately forthcoming, no beating around the bush, no sidestepping the question. "Brute's a member of my husband's motorcycle club, the Rebel Wayfarers, has been for probably six years." Bex thought about seeing the bikes riding up her street, the patches on the back of the leather vest he wore and she nodded. "He's a good man, one of the best guys I know." Ruby continued talking, moving them through the parked vehicles towards Bexley's car. "He's not had an easy time of things after he got home from overseas, as I'm sure you can imagine." *Right. The scarring.* Ruby was

78

talking about that piece of him that held little to no importance in Bex's eyes. Ruby stepped to stand in front of Bex, swinging to a stop, underscoring her words with this movement. "He's a good friend of mine, and I won't stand to see him played."

She stared at her sometime friend for a minute, and her confusion must have been evident on her face because Ruby burst into laughter, curly red hair bouncing with the force of the hilarity pouring from her mouth. Ruby leaned in, putting a hand on each of Bexley's shoulders, pulling her close and hugging her. A moment later, the laughter died out, and she heard Ruby say, "That's my Bex, our Brute's girl, not an ounce of dreadful in her. You're nothing but goodness, straight through and through."

"I don't know what you mean," Bex whispered, wrapping petite Ruby round with her own arms, holding tight for a minute.

"I know you don't, and that's what I mean." Ruby's words were perplexing, and Bex frowned, huffing out a little sigh. "But I really do want to know how you met Brute, so now, we're gonna hit the coffee shop and you're gonna dish like nobody's business, darlin'."

"It's…" Bexley let her words die off for a second, then picked back up, still not quite sure what she wanted to say, "…um, kinda…complicated."

"Oh, I'm sure. I'm sure it is." Ruby laughed, turning to point Bexley towards her car again. "You're driving. I had Slate bring one of the boys over. They already took my car, so you're my ride, Bex."

BRUTE

He looked down at the text message on the screen of the phone lying on the countertop. Brief, informative, and as she intended, it served as a quiet reminder of his promise. **This is Bexley**. Nothing more, no quips, no jokes, no smiley faces carved from characters. Just her name, as if she thought he received a thousand texts a day and hers would be lost in the masses. **This is Bexley**. As if he didn't already have her programmed into his phone. As if he hadn't picked it up every day, opening her contact information, staring at the stolen picture assigned to her name. Soft light shining through her bedroom windows streaming across the bed, head nestled into the pillows, hair a wild and beautiful halo, chin turned to one side, facing the camera, lips parted, sleeping sweetly.

Leaning deep, he put his elbows on the countertop, pressing his face into his palms, trailing his fingertips across the planes of his cheeks and forehead, testing the tenderness of the skin. Palpating the tiny points of pain, exploring the buzzing sensitivity, each touch glided gently across the uneven surface. Bulldog had worked a number on him, explaining as he went what he saw happening in Brute's face. Distortion hiding underneath the living grafts, there were layers upon layers of scar tissue, adhesions formed in unintentional places, twisting the surface. Muscles already damaged by the burns strained beyond what they would sustain, constant tension setting up an inflammation cycle that only worsened things.

Speaking aloud as he explored across the muscles and tendons, the doc said some things new, some things already known. Brute would never be handsome again, not a surprise. If the injury happened today, things might be different, but it hadn't, and things were the way they were. Nothing stayed inert, suspended in place, waiting for the magic wand to be waved. But Bulldog did think he could lessen the pain, ease the constant pull and sting of the scars.

Bexley, for a second time, appeared so immune to the damage on his face, it was as if it didn't exist. Simply didn't make a difference for her. Even surrounded by women who edged back from his path, who sucked in shocked breaths, muttering about what they saw, not bothering to hide their words in quiet, "Oh, my God, did you see his face?" Bexley ignored them and appeared to only see him. As she had in the grocery store, standing amidst boxed dinners, she did not shy away from him, from looking at him...from touching him.

Staring down at his phone where it rested between his elbows, he read the text again. **This is Bexley**. No demands, no requirements. She hadn't said, *Call me tonight or don't call*. Hadn't said, *Only call me if you want to go out*. No restrictions, the only limitation the one in his promise. A boundary he set for himself. *I'll call you tonight*.

It was tonight.

He twisted to look at the closed door to his guest bedroom. Natty had retreated there not long after they'd got home, begging off food in favor of resting. One look at her face, and he hadn't argued. Exhaustion was stretching its own kind of mask across her features, the extreme emotion endured today taking its toll. Looking in the other direction brought the darkened doorway of his bedroom into view. Living room or bedroom? Was this a conversation that needed privacy? They hadn't required it today, lost in each other within moments of sitting down. Their conversation not purposefully light, nor intentionally heavy, they'd simply shared and took from the other.

Picking up the phone, he stared at it for a moment, focusing on the time. Nearly eight. Late, but not too late. Tomorrow was a workday for her, but even if she had early appointments, he knew they wouldn't start until about ten o'clock. He could call now, and if they talked for an hour, which he thought would be a stretch, she would still have ample time to rest.

Picking up the phone, he wondered, *Why am I so nervous?* Without giving himself time to back out, he tapped her name, then the phone icon, listening as it rang once, then a second time, then a third before a young male voice answered, "Snow shoveling done cheap, keep the Dunk in mind this winter."

This greeting replaced hello, and he heard Bex in the background laughing, that laughter nearing the phone and before he could respond, her voice in his ear, "So sorry, this is Bex. How can I help you?" He couldn't answer for a moment, a long moment broken by her voice. A voice gone softer, sweeter, quieter when she called his name, "Brute?"

"Yeah." He barely got it out, so tightly had his throat closed. Laughter in the background, distant now, it sounded as if she'd moved away from Duncan. Privacy? Would she want privacy with him? Her sleeping face flashed through his mind, and he realized she didn't know how well he might know her. She'd solved the kissing thing fast, but who could forget his face, and her relief when he acknowledged it showed she wanted him to remember, wanted it in the open. But the rest? Did she know?

"I didn't know if you'd call." These words were spoken so small and quiet they could have been missed, her voice filled with such trembling fear and anxiety he shot a glance to Natty's door, wanting to be in two places at once. Needing to reassure two women he loved that he was there for them. He didn't flinch when his brain supplied that word, having long ago come to that realization of what his feelings for Bexley were built on. Love at first sight, something out of a fairy tale and then she derailed his brain by saying, "I'm so glad you did." Laying it out there for him, making it clear she wanted to hold onto what they already had after—as far as she knew—only two encounters.

"Bex," he murmured, and silence fell between them. In person, it would have been fine because he could see her face, read her emotions, her thoughts, but over the line like this, he had only memories to wind through his head. Determined to keep her on the phone, desperately afraid she would close down and hang up, he began talking. "Natty's asleep. We got home, and she went straight to bed. I haven't eaten yet, can't decide what to do for dinner." Stupid topic, food, but Natty was important, she'd know that. He had to push on, find a thread. "I live in an apartment so the kitchen isn't big, but the building is pretty new, so at least it's decent." He would keep throwing information out there, waiting until she found something she wanted to engage with and then he would set that hook, asking questions, feeding info back to her in an effort to pull more from her. "I like to cook, have a friend who's a chef and he's taught me a few things."

"I like to cook, too," she tossed this tidbit into the flow, and he latched on.

"You have to tell me what you cook. I'm more Midwest American, but can manage a mean Mexican casserole that doesn't always fail."

Laughter in her voice as she said, "Duncan, that's my nephew, my brother Brice's boy, he's flat out determined to eat pigs in a blanket every night for the rest of his life, so I can do those in my sleep." He chuckled, and she paused, then went on, a little breathless. "I do a lot of sweets, and at Christmas? Watch out. I'm all about making candies and chocolate dipped *anything*." He knew that about her, had seen her carrying jars and tubs of homemade treats to her car, delivering them house-by-house to her friends. Hadn't tasted. Not yet.

"I like sweets," he offered and heard a catch in her breathing so he pushed it, "and that sounded like a promise of holiday snacks to me."

"We don't have to wait for Christmas." Soft and slow, the desire to please him dripped from the words tripping off her tongue. "Can be for Christmas or for every day." He'd made a sideways appeal, and she gave him back the even stronger desire to deliver on that request if he would only promise he was staying. When she started talking, he could almost see her head tipped back, staring at the ceiling as she mentally ran an inventory of her kitchen. "I need cocoa, the bitter powdered kind, not for warming up after a snow, not that it's snowing now, but cocoa makes the dipping chocolate so much better. I can go to the store tomorrow—"

"I'll go with you." He interrupted her, wanting to have that with her. Wanting to kill the disappointment that rushed through him every time he pulled up in front of that building, the bitter part of the memory of that single kiss sending him to different stores for months before he could let the sweetness of it stay, setting aside the frustration as best he could.

"Okay." Her acceptance of his offer as immediate as anything he could have ever wished for, hoped for…dreamed. That eagerness pushed him on, flogging him forwards even as he might have tried to halt his response, bridle his tongue to control it, to keep his dreams underneath a glass case. Kept like a treasure, visible, but just out of reach, a clear separation maintained between what was and what might be.

"I'll pick you up?" Her two-toned response telegraphed a nervous, closed-mouthed nod, and he smiled. "Okay. Duncan staying over?" Another humming answer tipped the corners of his mouth upwards again. "I'll come early, we can drop him at your brother's on the way?" Silence met that question, and he froze, physically locking in place as the sure knowledge that he had pushed too far beat at him.

Then her, "That would be perfect," allowed his muscles to unclench, gave him space to breathe, gave him room to respond.

"See you at seven?"

This was as much a prayer as a question, and she answered both when she said, "Don't hang up. Don't go. Unless you need to, you told me you hadn't eaten yet, I'm sorry—"

"Bex," he interrupted, "I can stay on the phone as long as you'd like."

Soft, gentle, breathed, "Oh, good." Not afraid for him to know how much that meant to her.

"Did you make pigs in a blanket for Duncan tonight?" Conversational gambit, bringing her back to comfortable, he set the tone for the next hour as the give and take of water-testing flowed between them. At one point, she gave a tiny, ladylike grunt and he grinned, asking, "What in the world are you doing?"

"Climbing up so I can sit on the countertop," she tossed back with humor in her voice. "I'm on my feet a lot. I do hair for a living—" And they moved to more personal information sharing. Balancing what he already knew against what she told him, he was pleased she didn't hold much back, giving him an honesty and openness he didn't know he needed from her until that moment.

She was funny, so she gave him more, too, filling in the pieces he had often wondered, but never had a chance to know. Like the conversations he'd seen her have with people in her chair. Clients who would say something, feed her a line that caused her head to tip back, open-mouthed laughter rushing out of her. A silent movie from where he'd straddled his parked bike, but beautiful to watch. "—and he asked for a shave. Twelve-year-old kid, asked for a shave. I told him I'd have to charge him a finder's fee in order to shave him."

That dragged loud laughter from him, laughter that slowly died off in a good way, stilled by even more pleasure when she whispered, "God, you have the best laugh." Then she broke the news to him that she had connected every dot that lay between them, trailing them around corners and through the shadows, her words striking fear deep in his belly. News looking for a home, unsure if it would be welcome or not. "I only ever heard you chuckle before. I loved that, loved the sound. This—" She paused for breath, the sound of her deep inhalation triggering one of his own, a sympathetic bracing. "—is so much better, Brute."

Then she took it further, her mother-may-I steps covering broad sections of ground when she said, her voice gentle and soft, "I can't wait to see it." A quivering inrush of air, fear trembling on the breath that sustained her, then another. She was waiting, and he couldn't let her down, couldn't leave her out there on that ledge alone. Not his Bexley. *Not my girl*.

"I got no doubt you'll experience it in person tomorrow. I can't be sure until I see you, but think I could safely promise a chuckle. You're fuckin' funny, woman." Reassurances that he was looking forward to their trip, looking forward to seeing her, being with her, sitting next to her. "I like listening to you laugh, too." Voicing his prayer, he was asking for her to be comfortable and easy with him. Not that she'd ever been otherwise, but his hope stumbled there, waiting.

His girl handled his fears with as much care as he took with hers, easing the landing when she said, "I seem to laugh a lot with you. My face hurt today from laughing so hard." She didn't stutter, didn't hesitate, never turned a second guess to her words about her face, didn't mentally compare it to his, wondering if her words were callous or unkind. "I like to laugh. Belly laughs are the best." And with that, they had moved onwards, not looking back at what other people would see as a barrier to the kind of flow real communication demanded.

"Tell me your favorite thing to do." This was a question without a known answer, one of the few he'd posed so far tonight. So many options she might choose flickered through his head, moments captured as images, similar to how his brother Hoss explained his painting process. Snapshots, he called them, and Brute could see that. A flipbook of memories suited him better, and he glided past baseballs and park playdays, gardening and fashion shopping, wondering if her work would play a part.

"Ever, or right now?" In asking for the parameters of the demand, she attempted to ensure she gave him what he was looking for, she just had to sort out what that was first. Until she posed the question, he didn't know it mattered, but found upon consideration it did because he hadn't been part of her life before, not that she knew at least, so asking ever would remove the possibility he would rank a mention.

"Right now." *Why did I whisper that?* He wondered at the quivering in his belly, shaking his head as he turned his gaze downward. Waiting. Impatiently waiting for at least a second before she giggled. Tinkling music in his ear, trills of pleasure on the air, light and carefree.

"My favorite thing to do right now? Does it have to be something I've done?" An interesting shift in the question's definition, but saying it had been done would limit her answer even more than he'd considered before.

"Anything you want, Bex. Tell me what's your favorite...anything. Past, present, future. If it matters to you, it'll matter to me." If he had a chance, he'd put that promise into action, handing her seconds and moments to build that future with her. Keeping her present for himself, too, circling her round with nothing but Brute.

He got a soft hum, low and sexy. Smooth at the same time it vibrated with a raw want so carnal he went from half erect, a state he stayed in when thinking of Bex, to blood-filled and engorged, ready to fuck hard. Like a preteen staring at titty magazines in the basement, his hand cupped his cock through his jeans, fingers teasing the shaft as his breathing rolled rough and fast. Then she whispered to him, as soft as her hum...no, this was softer, gentler. "*I'd like to do you.*"

Tiny and fragile, she handed him her desires, and he took them in, ate them down, and gave it all back to her. "God, Bexley. The things you say. It's a good thing there're blocks and streets and walls between us, or I'd be in your bed so fast I'd beat you there." A stroke and the muscles in his arm bunched, blood pounding through his veins. "You want to do me, sweetheart?" Voice low, it filled with an edge he tried to hide. "You want to tell me what you want?"

Her words were gentle, but the blows landed as hard as the head of a hammer, beating into him. "I didn't know if you'd be interested." *How could she not know?* He'd made it clear as he could, clear as he knew, offering his time and attention. Then he listened as the real reason for her fears surfaced, the fault line in her confidence, his eyes darting to look at the still-closed door to his guest room. "You have to know why I was at group today. And some guys think—"

Interrupting her, he cut her off sharply, his voice a cleaver severing the idea from reality. "I would never, not ever think less of you for looking for help, Bexley. It takes a strong person to admit they can't go things alone. Group or a talking doc, neither of those mean you're weak. I'd never think—"

Turning the tables on him, she burst out, slicing through his words with brutality. "No, I mean you know I was raped by my boyfriend."

Fuck. Confirmation Brute didn't want, didn't need, because he already knew it. Her appearance there today cementing his understanding of why she was controlled, even in her risk-taking. Controlled and thoughtful. Raped by someone she trusted, and no wonder that faith was now held tight. The pause between her words and his silence grew, pushing her to apologies again when none were needed. Not between them. Never. "I'm sorry. I thought you knew."

"Bexley." He started out quiet, soft, then as he spoke and gained surety in his words, his voice grew louder, filling up the space between them In a way he wanted her to know it would never be void again. Him and her, from here on out. She wanted to do him? He just wanted her. All of her.

"Nothing could change the way I feel right now. The way I felt today, which was far beyond fortunate to be sitting and talking to you." Time to go all in, show her everything he had been holding back, make certain her fears didn't find any fertile ground in which to root. "The way I felt when I carried you home from New Haven." No need to name the bar, she would know. A memorable night for them both, his words an acknowledgment of the encounter. "Angry and favored in the same breath, then awed at the beauty granted me." Her skin, silken and sweet, heated under his hands. Jealousy blooming at the sheets; sanctioned soft cotton given privileged permission to cover her.

"The way I felt when we kissed in the grocery store." Not taking credit for the kiss, nor making it something she'd done to him. They were both participants in the action, willing and eager. "Nothing could change how I feel. I'm not most guys, and I think you know that." She made a noise, and he paused a beat, then pushed on. "I like you. Liked your mouth. I want more of it, Bexley. More everything. Liked everything I've seen, everything I've heard from you. You make me happy. That's why I laugh around you when I never do that shit. Never laugh. But you make me happy. Just by breathin', you make me happy."

When he finished speaking, he waited. A beat later, she gave it all to him. Everything he could want when she said on a half-broken laugh, "Then I guess I need to keep breathing, huh?" Her jagged sigh joined in for a moment, matching the feel of that laugh, sharp edges of insecurity far too near her soft emotions. His feelings for her would be a shield, making sure she was protected.

"I'd like that, sweetheart. So yeah, you keep on keepin' on."

BEXLEY

Gaze focused on her toes, she watched them flexing and bending in her socks, feet dangling and softly bumping against the cabinet doors. Heel one and then heel two, back and forth, a solitary parade of one marching in place. The butterflies in her stomach vied for attention against the tingling between her legs, Brute's softly voiced desires finding an answering resonance inside her. Her head kept getting in the way of things, thoughts circling back to where they'd been today, and what she'd just told him. The only other person those words had been uttered to was her therapist, someone she paid to take things in stride, talk her through to the other side with evenly paced words and phrases. Brute didn't follow that route, but when had he ever seemed to do what she expected? *Awed at the beauty granted me.*

"—parents live out west. She drove straight here from the college. She'll be staying—"

Not even realizing when it happened, she let his tone soothe her, dropping the words from importance, giving her what she needed to work through the things in her head.

His sorrowful utterance of her name had meant one thing to her, then his silence said another. Following that, a blunt dismissal of her blame didn't make sense. Even the doctor said men mostly had one of two reactions, either anger or a misplaced guilt. The doc'd probably said more, but that was what Bexley had absorbed from that session. When Brute's response didn't fit either mold, it had led her to immediately wonder if instead of mattering, which would mean she mattered, his caring was only a reflection of feelings he couldn't express about Natty's experience. But he didn't stop there in the no man's land of uncertainty, didn't stop at all. With his strength, he carried them through to the other side of her revelation by making sure she understood his words spoke truly. *You make me happy.*

"—doing me a favor, really. I need to go to the grocery store in the worst—"

The wave of his words was larger than life, swamping her emotional deck with goodness. For weeks she'd felt a sizable sliver of shame lodged in her brain at how he had cared for her. Wasted moments she could have spent with him, not even knowing how she'd found him in the bar clear across town. Now he crooned sweet things to her, telling her she offered him something precious that night when all she could think of was the sick on her clothes and clean skin under soft sheets.

94

"—own hours, so anytime I need to go, I—"

"I hate I got sick that night." Her whispered hiss of frustration ate into the things he was saying, dissolving them slowly to silence as he listened to her. "I hate I missed a minute with you."

"Wasn't your fault, Bex. And I didn't mind caring for you. Was my privilege." He followed the kernel of her interruption, as soft and gentle, his words wrapping her in a gauze of careful. The things he wasn't saying didn't fit the puzzle, leaving holes in her understanding as big as the holes in her memory from that night.

She confessed, "I've never misplaced an entire day before." All of Saturday night to Sunday evening. Every hour was gone. But even their absence left a greasy anxiety behind. Dirt not removed but swept underneath the throw rug to keep company from noticing. Still there, and if it wasn't attended to, could damage the things used to cover it. "I don't know what happened." *I think I do, but I know it wasn't you*.

"Guy at the bar drugged you." He filled in a slot, tracks extending on either side of that stationary tidbit. She didn't know where to take this from here. *Why were you there?* "I got you home safely. That's the important part."

"Um—" The sound had hardly cleared her mouth when he started talking, circling and scratching to fill in the rest of the picture. Tracks ahead and behind the previous morsel filled and filled and filled to overflowing.

"First off, I don't want to have this conversation on the phone. I can't see you, can only hear what you give me, and that isn't nearly enough for me. Let's talk this through tomorrow morning, but you should know I've been around a bit ever since I met you in the grocery store. Guy drugged you, I saw it happen. I took steps to make sure you were safe." She could hear the shrug in his voice so stayed silent. Willing to give him the time to finish the picture, not wanting to paint him into a corner with her questions. "Took care of you, Bexley. Had to, had to see you safe, sweetheart." She liked that name from him, not the bizarre one her parents had saddled her with, but the tender love word. Sweetheart. *His sweetheart, maybe?*

Strained, he asked questions in rapid fire. "Does that tell you that I don't give a shit about you getting sick that night? That I was honored to be the one taking care of you? It wasn't a burden, nor a hardship. Can you wait for the rest, honey?" She knew tension was what had twisted his voice, heard it in each word and believed him, deep inside her. Trusted what he said, and drew from that, drew without shading her own inflection and understanding over the top, a painful red wash of emotion she could set aside for once. He asked again, "Can you wait, Bex?"

"Yes." Easier than she expected, she followed his lead in this, glad of the decision the instant she heard his relieved sigh. Easing them farther from the place he didn't want to visit. She would drive off a cliff before steering them back that direction. Extending the tracks back to safety, she asked, "I make you happy?"

"Happiest I've ever been. My whole life." Now the emotional wash was his, but the swirl around her heart was all colors of the rainbow, mixing to make something uniquely Brute. "You gettin' any of that back from me, Bex?"

"Yeah." She breathed surety into the sound, wanting him to know about the goose bumps roaming up her arms at the thought of making him happy. About the shivering quiver traveling down her back to the idea of making him other things. Before she could say anything else, Duncan called from the other room.

"Auntie Bex." Dunk's voice declared tiredness, the edges of the sounds in his speech jangling up against their neighbors so they flowed together in a complaining blend of exhaustion. "Past bedtime for me."

She knew Brute had heard when he muttered, "Fucking shit, three hours." Eyes to the clock on the front of the coffeemaker, she silently concurred. Not on the expletive side, but on the "God, I can't believe we've been talking that long already" side.

"Be right there, Dunk." Mouth thoughtfully angled away from the phone, she didn't try to make excuses when she moved the device back into place. Just said right out how it was. "Barely eight hours before I see you again." Well, maybe that hadn't been what she intended to say, but his amused chuckle was worth any embarrassment she might suffer from her own forwardness. "I have to go, Brute."

"I know, sweetheart." That word again, and she decided it worked coming from him. *Sweetheart*. "Rest well when you get there."

"I will." Her promise to him was enough farewell, the call ended with disconnection without a good-bye, silence on the line for now.

Hopping off the countertop, phone tucked into her back pocket, she didn't know she was smiling until Duncan called from the doorway. "Who was that on the phone?" He had already ditched the jeans, pulling on a pair of the pajama shorts kept here for this kind of impromptu sleepover. He'd come over for dinner, but when time came for her to walk him home, he had wrinkled his nose, declaring he needed some Bexley time.

Not wanting to lie to her nephew, but not sure how to broach the topic of his favorite aunt maybe possibly dating without doing so, she said, "A friend." Hand out, she ruffled his hair, tugging him close so she could drop a kiss to the top of his head. *Another couple of years and he'll be too tall for this*, she thought, poignant awareness filling her that their time together like this was limited. "Bed turned down?"

"What kind of friend?" Rounding her waist with his arm, he gave her a hug before pulling away, much too soon to suit her. Refrigerator door open, he stood in the time-worn pose of all males when presented with food decisions. "Glass of milk or piece of pie?" Head down, hand on one hip, other hand holding the door open, he allowed chilly air to escape, flowing across the floor, teasing along her toes with a draft.

"Well, duh." She laughed, ignoring his other question as she pulled down glasses and plates. "Both." Time enough to mention who would be picking them up in the morning, explain who Brute was in a way that Dunk would understand.

BRUTE

He stood, staring at his truck. It was nearing seven, and he'd cleaned the cab thoroughly, but no amount of cleaning would change the fact that his vehicle was one most classic models would call a kissing cousin. Aged and worn, it looked exactly like what it was, transportation of last resort. *Why did I offer to pick her up?* Hand to his pocket, phone in his fingers, ringing in his ear followed by a sleep-roughened, "Jesus, brother. I must love you if I'm pickin' up at this hour."

"Gunny." Brute swallowed hard. "Need a favor."

Twenty minutes later, he heeled his kickstand down in front of her house. Unsure of the reception his idea would receive, he strode up her walk and towards the tiny porch where he'd watched her spend so many hours. Before he got to the steps, her door was flung open from the inside, and he heard a boy's voice, "Saw-*weet!* You didn't tell me he had a bike!" Duncan bounded through the opening, coming to a teetering stop on the edge of the porch, so engrossed in looking at the bike he didn't notice Brute's hand on his belly to stop his fall. "That's so cool!"

Duncan's neck twisted, and even from the elevated surface of the porch, he looked up at Brute, the beauty of his aunt shining through, showing their shared heritage. He recoiled only a little when his gaze fixed on Brute's face, then proved the adage of kids and honesty true when Dunk blurted, "What happened to your face?" A second later his filter caught up to his mouth, and he shook his head at himself, muttering, "Jeeze. Oh, man, sorry, mister, that was rude." Eyes to the floor, then to the bike, Duncan was trying and failing to recover until Brute responded.

"I got hurt in the war. A bomb. Doesn't hurt much now, looks way worse than it feels. Don't sweat it, little man." Make a connection, or leave things however Bexley had to have explained them? "You seriously offering to shovel snow?"

Chin lifting in surprise, Duncan stared at him a moment before a slow grin spread across his face. "You called last night." Not a question, the statement was a precursor to a teasing tone as Duncan lifted his voice, calling in a sing-song over his shoulder and back into the house, "Auntie Bex, your boyfriend's here." Shoving his hand out, Duncan gripped Brute's paw as soon as he lifted it from his side. "I'm Duncan, your friendly neighborhood snow machine and best nephew ever."

Brute hesitated. Which name should he offer to the boy? The decision taken from his hands when Bexley called from inside the house, "Ask Brute if we're taking my car to the store." Less than a dozen words gave even more evidence that she was as easy as he'd need her to be. He told her he'd pick her up, but when he showed on a two-person vehicle, she offered to keep their plans alive with alternative strategies.

Eyebrow cocked in question, Duncan waited for his answer. "Actually, I thought we'd walk you home. Then your Aunt Bexley and I can take the bike for a ride before we go to the store. I have a friend who can pick up the groceries and deliver them, so I got that piece covered." He tilted his head, liking how Duncan grinned up at him, the smile taking over his face in anticipation of his aunt's activities. "You think she'd be okay with that?"

An hour later, Brute and Bexley were sitting at a table with coffee cups in hand, staring out across the moving blue expanse of Lake Wawasee. Grocery store errand still in their to-do path, but after Brute'd received updates from Ruby on how things were headed with Natty, he had felt free to sidetrack Bex for at least this long. Especially after finding out she'd never ridden on a bike. From the dreamy look on her face when they pulled up to this dockside diner, she was a fan.

Conversations on the bike were necessarily limited, even if he'd held their speed to the sedate side of just over legal. Once they were out of the stop-and-go of the Fort, she'd gotten quiet. Feeling her nestle up against his back, arms around his waist and the firm lines of her thighs pressed to his hips, he hadn't wanted the ride to end, and neither had she. Balancing the bike between his legs, he'd stretched out his hand to assist her dismount in the lot and been surprised when she instead squeezed him tightly. Mouth to his ear, she'd whispered, "I understand how you can fall in love with something like this. Thank you, Brute, for giving me the chance to see the world through your eyes."

Only a few speedboats puttered across the water's surface. He knew that the standard fleet of pontoons and pedal boats would be back on the water once the weekend rolled around, getting in some late season lake time. Seated in a side-by-side position, conversation between Brute and Bex waxed and waned naturally as the view took their attention. There was a staggered height to their formation, because she was ass to the table, feet on the seat next to where he sat. He was leaned back, elbow to the tabletop propping him up, and the position and sun on his face felt good, but the best part was how she'd pressed into him, leg against his arm heating him in a very different way.

Without preamble, she asked nearly the same question as Duncan, but in a musing, "I want to know all about you" tone, instead of Duncan's shocked pain. "What happened to you, Brute?" Not a secret, nothing this visible could be, and he didn't mind her knowing since the delay of the question said it wasn't important to her except as it mattered to him.

"Roadside bomb. Wrong place, wrong time. Docs did everything they could, but it was a lot of damage." No need to catalog the number of surgeries, the time spent in hospital both overseas and here, the countless graft procedures, the—

"Does it hurt?" Her voice was gentle, the tone searching. She wasn't asking about the past, but looking towards the now. No need to dig up history for his Bex.

"Yeah, sometimes. Nerve damage." He shook his head and inclined sideways, angling in to her slightly, pleased when she leaned in to him even more. "Started seeing a new doc yesterday. He's using different techniques, new things. Gonna try and make it easier to deal with." Staring at the water, he hadn't seen her move so the barely-there touch on the back of his neck startled him. Her fingers started a slow up-and-down slide over the tense muscles there. When he tipped his head down to show appreciation, she dug the pad of her thumb into his flesh, rolling and working at one of many knots she'd found.

Soon she was leaning far sideways to rub and massage his shoulders. "Dang it," she muttered, and he lost the heat of her hands as she shifted around. A moment later, he felt her knees on either side of his shoulders; she'd moved behind him, spanning his width as she had on the bike. "Your muscles are tight all over." This was also muttered, and he grinned down at his lap when she continued, "Everything I feel is hard."

To tease, or not to tease? To tease, definitely. "You haven't felt everything, Bex." Her inrush of air told him she hadn't realized her words. He pushed it with what she could take as a promise. "Yet." Heat against his sides meant she'd tried to squeeze her thighs together, and he wondered if she'd be squirming in her seat if she was alone. "What time is your first appointment?"

A sigh told him he was right to bring them back down to reality. "Ten thirty. What time is it now?" He dug out his phone, woke it, and showed the display to her over his shoulder. Eight fifteen. "Do you…?" Sudden shyness gripped her words, her voice quivering for a moment as her hands stilled. He heard her swallow before she began again. "Do you want to go back to my house, Brute?"

"More than anything, Bexley." It was his turn to pause, controlling the rumble that threatened to break free. "You claimed a wish last night, and I very much want to see that come true. Want to grant it for you in all the best ways." Her legs tightened again, as did her hands; thumbs cupping the back of his skull, tips of her fingers stroking the scarred skin of his temples. "But you promised something, too."

"I did?" It seemed she asked the question in genuine confusion because he felt her body move with the shaking of her head, the shadows on the ground in front of them giving him a glimpse into her movements. "What did I promise you, Brute?" Hope and fear warred for space in her words, and he didn't know why.

He licked his lips before replying, his voice echoing low and sounding needy even to himself when he said, "Sweets." He watched as her shadowed-self threw back her head, hair flying. Laughter filled the air around him in a way that he knew would addict him after only this single exposure. "Gonna renege on that promise, sweetheart? Deny me something sweet that I want so badly?" She was the sweet he desired. She was the single thing he needed.

"Never!" She threw that word down like a gauntlet, daring him to question her resolve.

"Then we still have to hit the grocery store." He moved, ready to rise to his feet when he felt her palms on his shoulders, holding him in place. "What is it, Bexley?"

Her hands slipped down his neck, thumbs underneath his jaw, tipping his head backwards so he looked into her face upside down. She was staring into his eyes when she leaned in, and he lost their gaze as her head tipped to the side so her mouth could brush against his. This was just as chaste as the months-ago kiss, but she lingered for a long moment, then her lips moved against his when she said, "Thank you."

Brute straightened and twisted around, forcing her up so she leaned over him, not into him as he asked, "For what?"

"For making this so easy." She stared at him, a soft smile making her features radiant. "For being you."

"That's all I can be, sweetheart. With me"—Brute gestured towards his chest—"what you see is what you get."

"Then it's good that I see what I want." She laughed, rolling her eyes, talking through her laughter, "God, that sounded stupid."

"No, sweetheart. Not stupid." He reached up, capturing her chin with his thumb and finger, tugging her down for another soft lip touch. "Not at all stupid knowing you want what you see. I don't think so, anyway." Brute stood and looked down at her, fingers angling her face upwards now. "I see what I want, too." Her lips parted on a soft gasp, and he couldn't have stopped himself if he tried, so he gave in to the desire carrying him forwards, leaning down and capturing her mouth.

Moments stretched as he kissed her. With movements unhurried and deliberate while at the same time urgently driven by impulse, he slanted his head, deepening the caress of his lips against hers. Stroking into her mouth with his tongue, he consumed her, finding the caramel flavor of her latte worth pursuing. He groaned down her throat when her arms twisted around his neck, pulling him deeper into her, showing him with no hint of hesitation that she wanted more. Panting, he broke the kiss, burying his face against her neck, feeling the heat from her rolling across his skin. No less short of breath, she curled into his chest, nuzzling him and giving him an extended dose of her touch. Something he could get used to. Something he found he wanted more now than ever before.

He muttered softly, "Jesus, sweetheart," feeling the pounding of her heart where his lips had latched of their own accord onto her neck. "I could do that all day, kiss you until the sun drops behind the horizon."

"Me—" She took a breath that shimmied in the middle. "—too."

"But you gotta work, and I do, too." Her arms flexed and tightened, a physical rejection of the separation she knew was coming, and his body agreed with hers. Knee to the seat, he leaned in to her, feeling her legs part so he could slide closer. Mouth working up her neck, he trailed kisses along the edge of her jaw until he reached her lips. "I'll need another taste of you before we go, though." At his whisper, she arched her back, pressing her front to his and turned her head, offering him everything he wanted at that moment.

He took it all, and found in taking what he wanted, he gave in to her desires, too.

BEXLEY

"When did you start going out with Brute?"

Duncan's question was a surprise, and her jerking reaction caused the eggs she had been briskly beating with a fork to slop over the edge of the bowl. Tipping her head to one side, she studied him out from underneath her bangs. Pointedly not looking at her, he was arranging and rearranging the knife and fork beside his plate. His brows were drawn together in a sweetly confused look that reminded her of Jean so strongly, it broke her heart to think of Brice seeing his dead wife's face on their son.

When she didn't reply, he made one final minute adjustment to the alignment of the silverware and then lifted his head, staring at her. "Auntie Bex?" Mouth twisting, he considered his words for a long moment. "You didn't tell me. Was it..." His voice dropped to a whisper, and she heard a thread of disappointment in his voice, "Are you ashamed of him? You know, because of how he looks?"

Bexley straightened, putting down the fork and bowl, wiping her hands on the towel lying nearby. "Come here, you," she called, holding out her arms. When he fitted himself to her, she wrapped him up, holding him tightly. "No, I'm not ashamed of him. Do you know how he got those scars?" Dunk's head moved back and forth, and she giggled. "He's a hero."

He was, too. The day she'd gotten his name, she had looked him up online, found that he had been decorated while still flat on his back in a hospital in Germany. His actions had saved many of the soldiers in the column because he had seen a suspicious arrangement of trash on the side of the road, and recognizing it for what it was, had called a halt. His movements to return to the truck had triggered the IED however, and the blast had thrown him more than fifty feet. Four men had died, two more wounded irreparably. Fifty-eight lived. "He saved a bunch of people, but then the bomb went off anyway. He was closest to it, trying to keep everyone else back. I'd never be ashamed of a man like that."

"I didn't think you would, but…" Dunk took a breath. "…you never told me." His tone accused her of keeping secrets, of not trusting him with important information. Questioned his place in her life.

"Dunk, I'm not ashamed of him, and I'm not ashamed of you, either." Pressing her lips to the top of his head, she said, "It's just…new. Kinda. Mostly." She gave him a squeeze and released, turning back to their meal preparations. "New, but not. I met him months ago, but we didn't stay in touch. I didn't even know his name until recently. Then he called one night, came over the next day, and we rode his bike. You met him before our first date. That's why he was picking me up. So I'm dating, but it's new." Bex let some of her nervous anticipation fill her voice as she bumped Duncan with her hip. "You think he likes me?"

"Duh." Now Duncan was laughing at her giddy happiness, and that was fine by her. "Only like a lot."

"Good." She dumped the eggs into the heated skillet. "You doin' toast?" Just that quickly, they had moved past his questioning his importance in her life, worried that she was either keeping secrets from him or replacing him in some way. His faith in her restored, and she reminded herself to have the same conversation with Brice because his reaction this morning had carried the same question of need. "I love you, you know that, right, Dunk?"

"Yeah," he responded, and she turned to see a grin on his face, "only like a lot."

"A lot, a lot," she agreed, digging in the drawer for a spatula.

"Auntie?" Quiet again, his trembling voice pulled her head up, and she saw his eyes were welling with tears. "I love you, too."

"I know." Swiping at her cheeks with the crook of one arm, she scolded, "Now stop that. Right in the feels.

You're gonna make me cry in the scrambled eggs, and we all know that the tears of a favorite aunt are super salty."

His laughter carried her heart soaring, something that until Brute, only Duncan had managed.

BRUTE

Chief's voice on the phone wasn't expected. "My friend. How goes it?" Brute hoped this surprise meant good things.

He leaned forwards in his chair, elbows on the desk as he answered, "It'd go a fuckuva lot better if I knew who'd hurt my goddaughter." All of his investigative efforts so far had turned up nothing. Whoever the guy was, he was a ghost. They knew more about who it wasn't than who it might be. It wasn't a student in any of Natty's classes, nor any of her professors. Wasn't any of the local sex offenders, registered or not. Chief still had two guys on campus, but Brute couldn't ask for much more than the week already given to the search. "You got anything for me?"

"I do." Short and terse, the response shocked Brute, and he sat straight, spine ramrod stiff. Unfocused gaze aimed at the wall, he didn't have to wait long for Chief to continue. "Your girl's smart. So smart, coming in as a freshman who'd taken college courses the last two years of high school, she was allowed to take classes normally reserved for upperclassmen. She did a paper in a psychology class that got the prof's notice. He submits one student paper per class for publication. Only one. And he chose hers." Chief paused, and Brute made an involuntary noise, needing him to hurry the fuck up because this seemed like background info that didn't matter, but he knew Chief. If the man felt this was important, then Brute needed to be patient and listen.

"Older, just coming back to school after a seven-year hiatus, there was a rich bitch in that class who had been riding the wave of being the smart gal on campus. Until your Natty came along." Fuck. Was he saying what Brute thought he was saying? "She didn't like that, paid a guy to come up from Salt Lake to, in her words, 'distract' Natty."

"*Jesus*," Brute ground out the word, hearing Chief grunt in response. "Are you fuckin' shittin' me?"

"Shit free. We got the guy, and no worries for you, he now lacks the equipment to ever do that shit again. Seemed the most permanent solution to my man, so he took it upon himself to make it so. But this woman…" Chief trailed off for a moment, then continued, "Her daddy's high and hot up in Wyoming politics, so dealin' with his darlin' daughter would bring heat on my club. That said, I do see a way to deliver a payback that fits the crime."

"Talk to me." Brute waited, and as Chief spoke, he felt the muscles in his face pull and tug, stretching as he grinned.

114

BRUTE

Brute watched as Natty opened the newspaper. Seated in her customary place at the table, head in hand, she was propped semi-upright on an elbow in order to spoon cereal into her mouth. This lounging position was a holdover from childhood, and it warmed him to see it. He was surprised when she sat stiffly upright before exclaiming, "Holy shit." Her eyes flickered to him, then back to the paper, then she smiled broadly. "Check it! Senator's Daughter Pegged for Predator at Sex Club." She flipped the paper around so he could read the blurry picture's headline for himself. He sucked in a breath at her next words, knowing what he knew about the setup that bought that headline. "She was in one of my classes. Biggest bitch around to everyone. Especially me." Natty snorted, then giggled, "Pegged." Her voice dropped to a mutter when she said, "I *bet* she got pegged."

Frowning, Brute stared at her. "What do you know about pegging?"

"Pappa Ricky." Natty grinned saucily, arching her eyebrows as she gave him a flip of her hair. "I have an inquiring mind."

"Jesus." He stood, pushing away from the table. "You know what? I don't need to know." Turning towards his office, he called over his shoulder, "Ruby picking you up today?" It was group day, and Ruby taking Natty had become part of their routine over the past few weeks. So it surprised him when she grunted in a way that could only be interpreted as a negative. He looked back, seeing her mouth was full but her head shaking back and forth.

Garbled by cereal and milk, she told him, "Bex." He stood stock still, his brain going at warp speed, considering and discarding responses. She swallowed and repeated herself, wrongly intuiting he hadn't understood. "Bexley's taking me." The silver of her spoon flashed in the overhead light, disappearing into an ocean of white, reappearing bearing the cereal company's idea of fruit-colored pieces of puffed grain. "I told her I have my car, but she insisted." Another dip into the bowl, and she chewed and swallowed again, gesturing with her now-empty spoon. "It's like they think I can't do this myself. Like I'm not capable of making it to the group."

"I can't be a hundred percent sure, but I'd bet anything that's not it, Natty. It feels more like they want to make something that could be hard, easier to bear. Maybe they remember what it was like to go to group alone for the first time, maybe they want a better outcome for you than they had, but I'm fairly sure them taking you doesn't say one thing about how strong you are." He was feeling his way through this, hoping he got it right because she didn't need to feel like an obligation. He knew exactly how that could undermine your confidence, and didn't want to think of Natty taking any more hits. "They know you're strong, a fighter. So it doesn't say anything about you, but everything about the kind of women they are. Survivors, who have compassion and need to serve someone who's in the same situation." As he talked, all laughter had fled her features, and even after he finished, she just sat there, staring at him for a moment.

"You think I'm strong?" Trembling voice a throwback to her early teens, with four words, she exposed the burden of fear and uncertainty he'd been hoping to keep from her.

Taking a deep breath, he promised, "I know you're strong." He could hold enough confidence for both of them, for as long as she needed. "I know it, Natalie. You and Ruby and Bexley, strongest women I know."

"I don't feel strong." A whispered confession, one he hated she shared while he was a dozen feet from her side because he wanted to wrap her up, keep her safe, lend her his strength. Going to her now would weaken the determination she needed to build herself up, so he rooted his feet and waited. "I don't feel strong at all." Her gaze darted around the room, ricocheting off reflective surfaces, finally coming to rest centered on his chest. Barely a whisper, her voice trembled as she told him, "I feel weak."

"You were raped." He had spent hours on the phone with Bexley over the past couple of weeks. Schedules hadn't cooperated for them to be together often, and every moment he was with her was consumed by their slow physical exploration. He wanted his hands and mouth on her every chance he got, and since those weren't frequent enough for him, he was unwilling to waste a moment. This meant that the phone conversations had been all about exploring the way their minds fit together.

One of the things Bexley had said, and he'd noted, was how it felt to hear someone acknowledge what had happened to her. So now, when Natty needed it, he couldn't shy away from giving her the same validation. "That's the vilest betrayal someone can do to another being. You survived it. You are finding ways to help yourself deal with the mental and physical fallout of having something like that be forced on you." Not a consensual act and his words would never give her any inkling that he believed her anything other than unwilling. The social and legal system seemed predisposed to shadow the victim with the blame pencil, and he would fight to the death before he allowed Natty to feel the weight of that implication.

"You are unbelievably strong, Nat. So when they offer to give you a ride for something like group, maybe that's them wanting a little bit of that strength for themselves. Give it to them, let them do this. You'll never know how much you might be helping them." He opened his arms. She needed no further invitation, pushing to her feet and crossing to him, letting him wrap her up. "Like you give me strength when you let me do this. Makes me feel like I'm helping, but really you're helping me because there's not a thing I can do to help take away your pain. Except hold you and tell you I love you, and give you shit about eating a kiddy cereal."

Muffled against his chest, her voice held tears when she said, "You forgot to give me shit this morning."

"Jesus, girl, you eatin' that kiddy cereal again?" His words held no sting, were more near a croon than anything else, like a parent with a precious child, telling them they were loved. "There you go, shit given."

"I'm glad you give a shit, Pappa Ricky." Finally. Fuckin' *finally*, he heard a thin thread of humor in her voice, and Brute smiled, counting it worth every effort.

BRUTE

"Brute!" Bexley called out as she came, shoving her face into his throat, her body strung tight and quivering as his hand moved with purpose between her legs. Arm banded across her back, he held her tight against him in her bed, feeling an addicting rush of satisfaction at bringing her pleasure. He was at her house for the first time in days, already half hard when she'd opened the back door at his knock.

Brute had greeted her with a kiss, and the way she'd melted into him revealed she had missed their time together as much as he had. He'd pushed the door shut with his foot, twisted with her in his arms, and pressed her against the hard surface of the door, all while she gave him everything. Tongue, teeth, sexy groans into his mouth, hands restlessly roaming across his arms and shoulders, arms twining around his neck—every action exposing her need and desire. "Sweetheart," he'd barely got out before abandoning words for sensations.

Drowning in her, he'd drunk in each movement and sound, relished the feel of her crushed between his chest and the door, how the scent of her inundated his senses, making him wild to have her...finally.

He'd lifted her, stalking through her house and up the stairs to the room that had so often starred in his dreams. No argument from her, the fluttering drag of her fingertips working to pull his shirt from the confinement of his waistband encouraging him without words. Words they didn't have breath for in any case, mouths fused tightly together.

Impatient, in a choreography driven by desire, he'd twisted and taken them onto the bed, the mattress jolting and bouncing beneath him as he'd fallen. Then he'd rolled to her, fingers finding their way to the heat at her core, tearing at the fastening of her jeans to shove his hand down inside, diving into her panties to discover slick evidence of her desire waiting. He had wasted no time in giving her what she'd required.

Now, knowing the urgency had been bled from her need, he could take his time. Curling the fingers of his other hand, he used the backs of his knuckles to stroke across the unbelievably soft skin of her cheek. The pad of his thumb trailing a different path across her neck made her arch and lift her chin, offering him access. Lips questing across hers, he sought and found the vibrating hum that told him she liked what she was feeling, too.

Long, heat-filled moments later, he pulled back, rolling his sensitive forehead across hers, each indrawn breath as ragged as when he'd run five klicks in basic with a full pack. "Hey," he whispered, not wanting to break their connection. "I missed you."

"Missed you, too," she returned in a tone just as soft. "A whole lot, Brute." Curling sideways, she kept her gaze on him, gauging his response and he'd know why with her next words. "I don't like spending that many days without you." A wash of protective warmth flooded through him, because with those words, she'd handed him trust, making herself vulnerable and knowing he would be there to catch her fall.

"How can we keep this deficit from happening again? Keep you topped up with alla me, sweetheart." Nuzzling her cheek, he laid a complicated pattern of tiny kisses on her skin, knowing she wouldn't recognize the word drawn by his lips. *Mine*. "Keep you from being without your Brute?" He cupped her sex, lazy fingers tracing the outlines of her, a rekindling arousal announced in the slow lift of her hips, bow in her spine, and the soft exhale from her lips. "Keep me from bein' without my Bex?"

A slow tensing of her muscles declared the importance of whatever she was about to say, so he stilled, trying to control his reactions. Husky with anticipation, her voice rippled across his senses, her whisper loud as a shout. "You could move in with me." Stunned, he kept himself locked down, never letting that stutter of his heart reach his fingertips, sliding and slipping through her folds, every touch teasing, and light. She'd proffered a change in their relationship, a huge step forwards, and one he wasn't expecting. He'd thought she might ask for dates, nights in to spend together, dinners with family, time to explore more how they fit alongside the other. Her offering up her sanctuary and requesting he relocate hadn't even been on the horizon for him.

Her hand lifted, curling around his wrist and she turned her head, cheek pressing into his palm, seeking comfort. Or using that connection to safeguard herself, preparing for rejection.

We haven't even fucked yet, raced through his head, that thought followed with a certainty buoying his soul that it didn't matter. Had never mattered, not since the first kiss. She was his. *And I'm hers.* "My lease isn't up for a couple of months." Her breath gusted across his fingertips, an unspoken, deep sigh of relief. Wanting to give her more, he fed her his first thoughts, a stream of consciousness that would reassure. "If Natty's stayin' in town, and from the school brochures layin' every-fuckin-where, it looks like she's stayin' around, I could talk to her dad, see if he'd be willing to take over the lease, give Nat time to look for a different place if she wanted."

A pause, then he put himself out there, knowing in his bones she wouldn't leave him hanging. "I could load up my truck tomorrow." His apartment was furnished. There was only one room of furniture that he'd need to worry about. He'd be leaving all the shared things for Natty, but doubted that'd be a hardship here. Brute hadn't fully explored Bex's house, so he hoped there'd be a space for his desk and equipment. "Only thing I need is a place to set up my office and phone system." She knew what he did for a living, they'd talked about the differences in their jobs. "I don't have to transfer services, just need a place to plug in."

"What time do you want to start in the morning?" No hesitation, that was his Bexley. She was all-in on the idea, wanting to lock him into the decision before he could back out. Never knowing that he didn't see himself ever pulling away from this thing with her. Not now he'd come to know his dream woman existed, was here, in his arms. *No way in hell will I be walking away from her*.

Leaning down, he nuzzled her cheek, hand slipping to the back of her head, fingers pushing into her hair. He tightened his grip, tilting her head, arching her neck so he could slide his jaw alongside hers. Mouth to her ear, he lapped at her lobe, tugging gently with his teeth. Playing, teasing, loving the sound of her open-mouthed gasps. "Not early," he whispered, pressing a kiss to the soft skin behind her ear. Lips to her neck, he sucked and nibbled, placing hard, trailing kisses over every inch of skin he could reach. "I got other things I wanna do early." Fingers of his hand slipping through the wetness she offered, he firmly sketched small circles around her opening. "Things I wanna do late." Angling his wrist, he slowly plunged his middle finger inside her, hearing her sighing moan in reaction. "Things I wanna do now." Gentle, short thrusts had her breathing shallowly, the material of his shirt tightening across his shoulders as her hands fisted in the fabric.

"I wanna be *here*." The word "here" was accompanied by a deeper push, his thumb tweaking and rolling her clit. "Wanna be inside you." Another roll and a plunge gave him the feel of her body arching up against his hand. "Wanna love you here." Withdrawing his finger, he quickly matched it to his ring finger and thrust deep. "Now." Another push and a roll. "Late." Her teeth latched onto the side of his neck, her cry muffled against his skin. "Early." Tight and pulsing around his fingers, he felt her climax building. "Want that?" Her hair moved against the side of his face, evidence of her eager agreement. "Want me?"

"God, Brute," she whispered, his name gaining syllables with the sound of her passion. "Please."

"Please what, baby?" Steady and patient, he fucked her with his fingers, waiting. Hips rising and falling with every motion, she showed him what she wanted, but he longed for the words. "Please what, baby?"

"You." Gasping the word as he doubled the speed of his thrusts, his activities hampered by the confining fabric of her jeans. "Want you, please."

Carefully removing his fingers then his hand from her clothing, he efficiently stripped them both bare. Then he spent the next minutes reacquainting himself with her curves, the dip of her waist, peaks on the soft mounds of her breasts. Where before he had been restricted by his own moral code to gentlemanly behavior, this time— God—this time, he had free rein to explore. Map out the things that turned her on. Map out his favorite places, plotting repeat visits even as he traced them with tongue and teeth for the first time.

Condom in place, he gently pulled her hand away from his cock. As he had explored her, she had been granted the same opportunity and hadn't wasted any time in familiarizing herself with his body. Fingers traced his muscles, and she'd rolled one nipple between finger and thumb, a sexy smile curving her lips when he groaned at the sensation. "Done playing, Bexley." Brute moved between her thighs, letting her hips cradle him, hard cock sliding up and over her clit. "You want me, sweetheart?"

"Yes." Spoken like a plea, he watched the tip of her tongue dart out to wet her lips and leaned down to capture her in a hard kiss that demanded every response from her. He sucked her tongue into his mouth, toyed with it for a moment, then thrust his between her lips, taking everything he needed, knowing each moan and gasp were her gifts to him. "*Brute—*"

Whatever else she'd been about to say was cut off when he shifted, shoving one elbow into the mattress as he reached down between them. Thumb to her clit, he rolled across it once, twice, stroking the engorged nubbin of nerves, the head of his dick thudding in a sympathetic response. Gripping his cock, he dragged the crown down and across her pussy, wetting the condom and then curved his back, hips pushing forwards as he thrust inside her for the first time. Slow and steady, he pushed deep, and without pause deeper yet, listening to her breathing, alert for any signs of discomfort. To the root, he locked into position there, keeping his cock buried inside her. The fluttering clenches surrounded him, her voice on the air around him, soft lips of her mouth to his ear as she called his name again, "*Brute.*"

"More beautiful than I imagined," he whispered. At his confession, her arms curved around his shoulders, legs around his hips and she held him tightly. Holding on, not pushing away. Not trying to escape. Wanting this just as much as he did. "Every dream fell short of this." He felt the first cracks in his façade break through, tearing apart the mask he'd been presenting to the world for years. This moment with her was something he had believed was never to be. Something he had never experienced, and never would, missing without understanding how profound the absence. All his chances torn away by war, the reality of his injuries had destroyed any fairy-tale ending.

But here she was. Unmistakable proof that anything was possible.

"So goddamned beautiful."

Anything. Even this loving surrender of a woman who wanted him proved there was life after death. That's where he'd been for so long, just a walking shell of himself, might as well have died on that sand. Proof in his arms, because his Bexley, who didn't care what he looked like, how his voice sounded, a woman who looked straight through the roughness of his scars wanted what they were building as much as he did. As beautiful inside as out, she ignored the horrors resting on the surface to brush past the thick veil that had kept much of the world at bay.

His camouflage had done so much more than merely concealing him. Without his knowledge, it had hidden this from him. All of this—a chance at living again, and the possibility of beauty like this in his arms. In his life. Masquerade interrupted, what had become a shroud was torn away by her actions months ago. Delicate chin lifted in the aisle of a common grocery store, and him not understanding that the soft caress of her mouth offered so much more than a kiss. This was more than his chance to keep her, it was a door opening, an opportunity to stay in the world in a way that would keep his soul alive. "My Bexley is so goddamned beautiful."

BEXLEY

Brute covered her, his forearms pressed deep into the mattress supporting much of his weight. His lips grazed the skin of her neck, soft kisses tracing the route he took to her mouth. Heat from his body enveloped her, branding her arms where they crossed his back. He filled her, the press of him inside so sweetly perfect she could have wept. *Everything I want, right here.* Over the past weeks, his lazy explorations of her mouth always left her wanting more, and now to have him, finally *have him*, was brilliant. With every inch of him buried inside her, he was the first man she'd wanted since that long-ago night. First man in years, and she never wanted him to leave.

Terrified when her mouth ran away from her common sense earlier, the question she'd asked had coated her in a fragile vulnerability so frightening it stole her breath. She'd been ready for any reaction except the one received. With that promise to bolster her courage, holding his words tight to her heart, she put her lips to his ear and urged, "Love me."

He groaned, his forehead coming to rest on her collarbone, sweat making their skin slick where they touched. With her palms flattened against the muscles of his back, she felt a stirring underneath his skin, then his hips arched back the smallest amount before plunging back down. That was when she felt him tremble. Belly to belly, she lay underneath him, and he was quaking, his whole body shaking, a reaction to their closeness that was nearly terrifying because she didn't know what to make of it.

Afraid he was in pain, she pushed the back of her head into the pillow so she could crane her neck around to see his face. His beautiful eyes were closed, scarred lids clamped tightly together, and as she watched a tear broke free, trailing along his nose, the droplet falling in a hot, wet splash onto her shoulder. "Brute." Her voice shook nearly as hard as his muscles did, not knowing what was happening. "Honey, what's wrong?"

"Nothing." Suspended in time, she waited, and he gave her more. "For the first time I can remember, nothing is wrong." Muscles in his thighs tightened, and she gripped with her legs, giving him room to rock out, and push back in. "Everything is right." The drag of his cock sparked something inside her as he pulled back again, farther this time, reaching the apex of the arc and leisurely gliding back in deep, nurturing that fledgling flicker. "You're right."

"Baby," she whispered, envisioning the spark flashing hot, catching fire, building, and found herself enveloped by a heat rushing through her chest so her throat closed around the words she wanted to say. His mouth touched her neck, lips slipping up the column to her jaw. "Honey, that's—" She lost track of the thought when he stroked out, and back in, managing somehow to hit every last nerve ending she possessed, stoking the fire higher.

Deeper. He moved over her, his body working to bring them along this road. Hips in and out, his back curving and hollowing in turns, face pressed to the pillow beside her head. The sweat-slick slide of his belly against hers felt like satin, while the grind of his chest against hers was like nothing she'd experienced.

"We're right." His grunts carried the weight of his belief with them, his hands moving, one arm shoved underneath her back, the other threading down so his palm cupped her ass. "I need you, Bexley." He nudged the side of her head with his jaw. She turned to meet his mouth with her own, opening for the onslaught of his tongue, tasting him, the dark flavor of his arousal painting her mouth with frenzied desperation. "Need you so much, sweetheart." Fingers tight on her ass cheek, he pulled her hips up to meet every downward thrust. "Can't lose you."

"Not going to," she whispered but wasn't sure if he'd heard. "I'm not going anywhere, Brute."

Mouth to hers again, the sound of their bodies slapping together filled the room, and the flame that had been rolling through her body became a bonfire, lifting her high. She tried to break the kiss because it was too much. Everything was too much. She was coming apart at the seams, and it was too—

Deep. So deep it seemed he was trying to bury himself inside her and she needed that connection as much as he did, her back twisting uncontrollably as he moved, shifted, and planted his mouth to the base of her neck, grunting as he plunged hard. Once, twice. Farther than she would have believed possible, and he convulsed in her arms, his entire body giving witness to the strength of the feelings moving through him. A final time, hard against her, deep inside her, and he groaned. In that cry, she heard her name, and her arms and legs tightened around him, holding him close. *Not going anywhere*.

BRUTE

He woke to a dream come true. Not fading away at the stroke of midnight, still in his arms, her even breaths music he had listened to through the night. Beautiful in repose, as he already knew, but this time his perusal of her sanctioned by her own words. "Stay," she'd told him, wrapping her arm around his chest, holding on as if daring him to try and dislodge her. Knee on his thighs, ankle tangled between his legs, she draped herself like a cover he would use every night if she agreed. And she had. He remembered every word of her question and his answer. Today would be busy. Calls and testing the waters with Natty, but he was certain she'd jump at the chance to regain independence. Then would come boxing things, and a single trip in the truck would carry all he needed here.

Our house. The tiny cottage he had watched and envied for so long because it held her inside. Neighbors to meet in time. Each moment bringing them forwards.

Rolling his neck, he brought his lips to her temple, pressing a kiss there along with a whisper, "I love you, Bexley." She sighed and nuzzled into his shoulder, her hair drifting across his skin.

I should get up and make those calls, he thought. Pushing at the covers, he threaded his way underneath with the arm wrapped around her. Palming her ass cheek, he caressed her gently for a moment. *Later*, he decided, dipping his fingers down along the crease by her thigh and down the back of her leg. Fingers behind her knee, he tugged and slipped it up his body. Fingers sliding back to her core, he traced along her folds.

Tiny movements and a soft moan signaled her rise from sleep. A rise matched with one of his own, the tent in the covers evidence that he would be ready when she was. Her head tipped, and he felt her mouth on his chest, teeth scraping across his nipple. "You awake, baby?" Her two-tone inflection familiar and sweet, told him she wasn't willing to disengage in any way. Hand to the side of her head, he swept her hair back, seeing her eyes roll up to look at him. "Bring me that mouth, sweetheart." Open lips, her tongue twirled across the flat disk before she pressed a kiss.

Then she was moving, that glorious slide of curves against his hard planes, and he used his muscles to good effect, positioning her where he wanted her. "Kiss me, Bexley." Voice unrecognizable, jagged and harsh, he watched her pupils dilate in response as his mouth continued on, unbidden. "Make me believe this is real. Not gonna disappear. That you're here. That I'm here, with you, in your bed." Her head lowered, mouthing seeking his. "That you want me." Lips fused together, she kissed him, tongue chasing his on a shuddering breath.

He believed.

Bexley

"You don't understand me, apparently." Bexley felt her eyes widen. She'd never heard Brute sound like this before, and even though it wasn't directed at her, the tone was still frightening. "You told me you had the guy. Told me your man took care of business in a way that the guy wasn't gonna forget. You came through on the promises of getting rid of the bitch, too." She heard the cupboard door open and close, the quiet clink of a coffee mug on the countertop, followed by the purring rumble of the coffeemaker.

Peeking around the corner, she saw him standing with his back towards her, looking out the window. "Now you seem to be telling me that we're not done. How'd you miss a second guy, Chief? Huh? Riddle me that." The weight of scorn in his words made the air heavy, and she dodged back, determined to head back upstairs before he saw her and thought she'd been eavesdropping. *It's his house now, too*, she thought, *and he's got every right to have whatever conversations he wants*. She stumbled on the first stair, her hand going out, slapping the wall to halt her fall. *Shit*.

Glancing over her shoulder, she found his gaze fixed on her. Then he gave her the truth of their relationship by not closing out the call, not changing the topic, not cutting back on what he was trying to communicate. His eyes stayed on her face as he lifted one arm, hand out, fingers curling invitingly towards his palm even as he continued the conversation. "I don't give a fuck what you thought two weeks ago, Chief. At this point, I don't care to point fingers or play the blame game. I just want Natty safe."

She sucked in a breath as she made her way across the kitchen, fitting her hand into his, letting him pull her close. Lifting her chin in what had become a natural movement, she offered him her mouth, and he took it, lips pressing to hers softly, lightly, then he nipped her bottom lip before giving her a final gentle kiss. These actions in direct contradiction to the severity of his tone were perplexing, and the comment about keeping Natalie safe concerning. Eyes to his face, trying to read his expressions, she let herself lean in to him.

Focus back to the phone, his arm wrapped around her shoulders as he said, "You're lucky, Chief." A pause, then he snorted in amusement. "Yeah, lucky. I got a beautiful lady wrapped around me right now, makes me a nicer man. Still, do not mistake my nice at this moment with something that'll happen all the time. You find me this guy, get me the info. Do not, and I'm not asking this but telling you, do not have your man take care of this one. If the other guy was the camera guy, that means this one is the rapist. You find him, and I get him. Got me?" A longer pause, then he grunted, his arm giving her a squeeze. "Yeah, she's beautiful." Another grunt, and it sounded amused. "Yeah, mine." A final pause, then a snort. "Later."

His arm tightened around her neck as he disconnected the call, shoving the phone into his pocket.

That one single word ricocheted around inside her head. *Rapist*. He'd been talking to someone about finding Natalie's rapist. Finding and meting out his own judgment. And not for the first time, if she had understood the measure of the conversation to which she'd been privy. He had sounded hardened, dangerous. And it sat in his mouth like it lived there all the time.

A memory of him riding his bike up her street flashed, her view of the other men with him revealing them to be equally as hard. Far from the manner of a man who'd carry someone home, spending himself to tend to an unconscious woman he didn't even know. Giving nearly twenty-four hours of his time to make certain she was okay. *He's both men*, she thought. Caring so deeply he would turn himself inside out to ensure those he loved were okay. Caring enough to take on whatever was needed to make sure that okay continued, moving on into better.

Hugging his waist, she waited, and when he didn't say anything, she asked, "Everything all right?"

"Fuck no," he responded immediately but stopped there.

Unsure of her place in the overheard conversation, this all seemed shifting ground under her feet, so she waited another minute, then let him know, "If you need to talk to me, you can." Muscles in his back shifted, and his arm tightened, squeezing and then relaxing again. "Is that coffee for me?"

BRUTE

As he handed Bexley the mug already prepared, Brute considered her. She didn't seem the smallest bit concerned by what she'd overheard, the conversation she'd walked into—tried to avoid, if he read things right, betrayed by a stumble. That lack of concern was troubling. He'd been open, not trying to hide the topic and marked each flinch and tiny sound she'd given as indicators to her comprehension. She understood as clearly as Chief what he intended to do to the man once he was found and secured.

I'll kill him.

The thought didn't give him pause, didn't lift even the barest ripple of remorse in his head. Watching Natalie struggle, knowing the reason was the action of a sadist wearing a mask of his own, it was the only acceptable response. It made him sick to imagine the rapist strolling through society as if he weren't an animal. Stalking past innocents on the street. Brute knew this was a predator who wouldn't stop with one. Brute believed in his gut that Natty wasn't the guy's first. Her story showed he'd put a great deal of thought into the when and how, which meant practice. If that were true, if the bastard had a taste for it, then no way in hell she'd be his last. First, last, somewhere in the fucking middle—none of it mattered. The man's family wouldn't factor. His profession not a concern. His potential gifts to humanity were not to be balanced against Natalie. Dead, he would offer value, and Brute would gladly plant the corpse where its decomposition would do the most good.

But he'd lived with this knowledge for a while now. Lived with men's death on his hands for years. Just causes didn't matter whether sanctioned or not.

Bexley had learned this side of him two minutes ago and then followed it with an offer to chat and a request for coffee. That didn't settle him, in fact, it moved him to the unsettled side of things.

So he considered her. No tenseness, her eyes weren't wide or frightened. Nothing that would give any indication that he'd been talking about anything more stressful than the weather. Not even that, simply a topic that needed no further discussion. Moving on.

He'd met Brice, had dinner with her brother and nephew twice now. Dunk had been a good buffer that first day they'd shown up before school, walking in side-by-side with Brute to demonstrate to his dad how comfortable he could be around a man with a monster's face. Dinner had been just as easy, Brice and Bexley working in tandem to make it that way. Even if she'd been clear that while her brother's opinion mattered in most things, where Brute was concerned, she wasn't seeking approval. And Brice went along with that.

Brice, whose sister had been brutally raped, didn't have a single hard inquiry for the biker outlaw his sister had hooked up with. Didn't question anything. No interrogation. No reservation. Brice just went along with it, and not on the surface, but in an all-in way. Brute hadn't thought about it except to give a sigh of relief that the meet the family part was behind him. The parents weren't a consideration. Bex had talked about how they'd moved on even before their kids were out of the house. So as long as Brice and Duncan liked him, he was in like Flynn.

"You ever tell Brice what happened, Bex?"

He got his answer when her flinch nearly took her out of his arms.

"Why, sweetheart?" Ignoring the hot coffee trailing down his chest, he tightened his arms. Something she'd said during their first call surfaced, and he asked, "You don't think Brice would understand, do you." Not a question, but her head nodded all the same. "Gonna take away the chance for him to redeem mankind?" She jerked again, and he unwrapped one arm to retrieve the mug, setting it aside. "He wouldn't believe you, is that it? Damn, and I liked him."

"Of course not." As he knew she would, Bex hotly defended her brother. "Brice knows me. He knows I'd never lie about something like that." She dropped her chin down, avoiding his eyes.

"Is he one of those guys who'd think it was always the chick's fault? Fuck." Brute shook his head. "You think he's teaching Dunk that shit?"

"Brute." Her voice was soft. "I know what you're doing." Her arms moved, palms sliding up his back, pressing in to hold tightly. "It's not that."

"Then what, Bex? He loves you, seen that with my own eyes. That love shining when he watches you or talks to you or talks *about* you. Why would you deny him the chance to help you?" Palms to her ass, he lifted, and she gave a hop, settling her legs around his hips. He turned, putting her on the counter, staying close. "Use all the tools you have to hand, honey. Before me, who did you call in the middle of the night when you had a bad dream?" In the weeks since he'd been seeing her, she had not hesitated at picking up the phone whenever she needed him, having no qualms about exposing her fears. She stayed silent, which was what he expected. "You didn't have anyone, did you? Made it through on your own."

Fingers curled under her chin, he ran his thumb across her bottom lip, pressing and toying with the plump flesh, slowly caressing with each side-to-side stroke. "Makes it even more precious that you talked to me, honey. Even more amazing that you trust me to keep you safe, trust me with your thoughts, with your uncertainty."

Bright blue eyes ringed with wet-clumped lashes, she stared at him. Without speaking, she said everything he needed to hear, because that steady look was filled with trust and love. "When Natty came to me, I took the burden of telling her folks from her. Talked it through with them, let them get the pain out of the way, so she didn't have to bear that along with her own. I knew their hurt would rip at her, but knew they had to know because there was no way she could keep that big a secret from them forever. For a time, sure, but not forever. That's too big a secret to navigate around for long. Made it so when she talked to them, it was all about support and love. Gave them a space to get their self-recrimination out of the way, so she didn't have to tell them what they already knew. She didn't blame them. Why would she, they weren't even there. But they blamed themselves because their baby girl needed them, and they *weren't even there*."

He paused, catching one of the tears that had trailed its way to her upper lip, using his thumb to stop it in its tracks. "Let me do the same for you, sweetheart. Let me take that on." Her lashes fluttered, and a torrent of wet covered his hand and wrist, tiny droplets of salty self-loathing, because she hadn't felt strong enough to tell her brother. "You don't have to do anything alone anymore, Bex." Leaning in, he brushed his lips against hers, and then took a chance at telling her how important this was, because by giving him this, she would be taking something from him, too. "And neither do I."

BRUTE

He watched Brice stand at the window, looking out to the yard where Bexley was paired against Duncan in a game of toss that would go on for another half an hour at least. Brute had timed things so Brice would have enough space to get himself under control before the two people he loved most in the world came back inside. Blue eyes so very like Bexley's had stared at him unblinking once he got past the introduction to the topic. No natural lead-in for this, and if the uneasy swallows Brice struggled with were any indication, it meant a match to the nausea and anger Brute had felt were welling in this man, too.

Still wordless at the end, Brice had stood and stalked on stiff legs to the window, taking up watch. Another ten minutes passed, and Brute let the silence remain, not knowing Brice well enough to predict what was going through his head, what he needed to process the information. Soon enough, Brice cleared his throat and asked, "She's seeing a doctor?"

"Yes." Bexley had given him permission to respond to any questions truthfully if he knew the answer.

"A good one?" Lifting one hand, Brice flattened his palm against the wall, and Brute watched as his fingers curled in of their own accord.

"Yes." That hand was now a fist, and Brute expected the next question, had been waiting for it.

"She tell you who it was?"

"Not a name, no. But it was a boyfriend." Cords ridged the back of Brice's fist, knuckles standing out in prominence. "In Oregon. Her senior year."

"Joshua Harpe." *Thank you*, Brute thought, filing away the name of a dead man. Taking a deep breath, Brice blew it out in a controlled stream, not turning away from the window. "I should have taken her with me when I left." He shook his head. "Should have been there." His clenched fist thudded against the wall. "She never said anything. I knew…when I went back for her graduation…but she'd been working and going to school, like always. Just trying to keep things together. Our parents were worthless." Another thud, stronger, heavier, the meaty smack echoing in the room. "If she'd told me…"

"You know now." Time to derail the anger before Brice unthinkingly turned it the wrong direction. "Question for you, Brice. And this matters, man. I love your sister. I like you, love Dunk. But she's my reason for breathing." At his words, Brice swung from the window, staring at Brute as if he were committing a social faux pas, bringing the topic of their discussion away from Brice's anger and focused instead on Brute's emotions for Bexley. "You thinking of blaming her for any part of this?"

"What? No." The headshake and words came simultaneously, and Brute nodded. "Why would you...?" Chest and shoulders lifting in a heavy sigh, Brice's head tipped forwards, and he directed his gaze at the floor. "No blame for anything. I'm just mad she didn't think she could tell me herself. Mad she's kept silent all these years. When my wife died, and I called, I did it knowing that Bex would be here as soon as she could. And she was." He lifted his head, unashamed to show Brute his emotions, tears trickling down his cheeks. "Hurts. Feels like I failed her because she didn't believe I'd do the same."

"That's not it, man. She didn't tell you because she couldn't. It wasn't anything to do with you at all. She couldn't bear being the one to cause pain." Brute shook his head, pushing up from the armchair. He crossed the floor to where Brice stood and reached up, gripping his shoulder. "She needed me to tell you. I'm just glad I was here to do this, man."

"Me, too." A shout from outside had both their heads swinging to the window where they saw Bexley on her back, hands up cupping one eye. Both men were moving to the door when a running-scared Dunk got close, and Brute saw her reach up, her trick working on her nephew,

147

pulling him near enough to tackle. Brice stopped and snorted a laugh. "Some things never change. She used to pull that one on me, too." He looked at Brute. "I'm glad you're here. She seems...comfortable with you." Narrowing his eyes, Brice asked, "You really love her?"

"I do. I'm a lucky man." Brute stared outside as Bexley struggled to her knees only to be pulled down by a determined Dunk who then started a campaign of tickles all his own, leaving Bexley's face flushed. Her kissable mouth grinned widely as she looked up to see them watching out the window. Lifting a hand to wave, her lips made an "O" of surprise as Dunk pulled her backwards, tickling now turning to wrestling.

"Yes, you are."

BRUTE

"Hey, Brute!" The shout came from across the backyard of the clubhouse and Brute straightened from checking the gas gauge on the grill. Today was the club's annual family barbeque and he'd shown up early to help with set up. Squinting against the glare of the sun, he tried to make out individual faces in the group of people coming out the back door. Red hair glinted in the bright light of late afternoon, and he grinned at Ruby as she made her way towards him.

"Hey yourself, Ruby. How you doin', honey?" He slipped one arm around her shoulders and gave her a quick sideways hug.

"Hands off my woman, motherfucker," Slate yelled, wrestling a cooler out the door and letting it drop with a thud to the ground. Brute stared at him without responding and tightened his arm again, hugging her close. "Fuck me," Slate yelled, shoving the cooler with a foot, pushing it to one side of the path. Brute felt Ruby shaking with laughter and he looked down to see her grinning at her old man. "No fuckin' respect."

"Full respect, Prez," Brute called, stepping away from Ruby. Bending to the grill again, he asked her, "Bex inside yet?"

"Thought she was coming with you?" As if they were strings on a marionette, Ruby's quiet words pulled him upright, and he turned to look down at her again, slowly shaking his head side to side. "Shit." She was already digging in her pocket when Brute rested a palm on her shoulder. "Brute?" He shook his head again.

"She needs me, she'll call." *I trust her. She knows how much I want this*. He did. Wanted her to be comfortable around the men who had started him down the path of living again. Wanted her to blend with his family, like he'd done with hers. "Natty's coming with her, so they're probably just runnin' late."

Natalie had started classes at the local business college. She was settling in, making herself a home in Fort Wayne and this made Brute happy. Not only did he get to keep his goddaughter close, but it meant his friends would be visiting often and he looked forwards to introducing Dylan and his wife to Bexley and her brother. And his brothers. Tonight would be the first time Bex would meet any of the men from the club. She hadn't seemed nervous about the idea when he left the cottage after dropping off a chattering Natty, but nerves could have struck either of the women at any point. He was still being careful with Natty, working to ease things for her as much as possible.

Busy with the grill, he tried not to count the minutes as they ticked past, still with no Bex or Natty. He flipped burgers for the adults, grilling hotdogs for the kids, and their national president's woman had already put in her order for a burnt dog. Twice, like she thought he'd forget. More likely she forgot she'd asked, knowing Willa. Brute grinned, tongs in hand, positioning another dog directly over the flames, watching as the skin started to crisp and blacken. A year ago he couldn't have done this job. Would have been uncomfortable so close to an open flame, hopeless connections in his head forcing him to the shadows of the gathering instead.

"Brute." He closed his eyes for a second, relief sweeping over him as Bexley's voice rang out across the space. "Come help me." Twisting, he felt Ruby's hand glance across his arm and knew she was as relieved as he was. Bexley was trying to balance two cake pans, one teetering dangerously to the side. "Shit," she grunted just as he got there, taking the pan from her slipping grip. She reached up, tucking the foil covering back into place over the corner of the pan he held, absently muttering, "Thanks, honey."

"What'd you make?" He grinned as Natty came through the door with another two pans in hand. Cooking was what the girls were doing today, having been assigned sweets by Ruby, and that being something Bexley liked to make, she had clearly gone all in.

"Stuff." She was muttering again, and he turned to see her glancing around the yard. About twenty guys had shown so far, half of those with women, or women and children, which meant there was a large group milling around. "Not enough, probably."

"Not the only one bringin' treats, Bex." He crowded her for a moment, causing her to tip her head back, looking up at him as he leaned in. Brushing his lips across hers, he returned for a second touch, pressing firmly. "You ready for me to introduce you around?" She already knew a small handful of women, mostly from the counseling group, but there would be more people here tonight. Bex nodded. "Wanna grab Natty?"

He took the second pan from her, waiting for a moment until she nodded again. "I'll be right back." Head lifting, he looked towards the clubhouse just in time to see Natty relieved of her burden of pans, too. "Natty, 'mere." They spent the next half an hour strolling from group to group, his two girls meeting everyone else who mattered in his life.

Standing beside one of the barrels filled with ice and cans of beer, Brute kept an eye on Bexley. She was sitting in a lawn chair, feet curled up, chatting with Sharon, Gunny's woman. Both women were smiling and laughing, and his sigh echoed Gunny's for being filled with relief.

"She's good, brother," Gunny told him, and Brute nodded. She was good. Life was good. "We're expecting again." Brute stared at Sharon, and grinned, because sure enough, she had a little belly on her dancer's frame.

"Boy or girl?" The couple already had a little girl, and watching Gunny with his daughter was hilarious. She might have been made of the finest porcelain the way he handled her.

"Girl. I'm so fucked, brother."

"Oh yeah, you are," Brute agreed on a chuckle. "You're fucked now, but just take a minute and think about life fifteen years down the road. Boyfriends and parties, learning to drive. All those things to live through. *Fucked*."

"Don't. I can't think about that. Give me this, brother," Gunny had adopted a pleading tone and Brute laughed. "*Jesus, Brute*." That was a guttural mutter and Brute glanced across to see Gunny looking pained, brows drawn together.

"What?" *What the hell?*

"Never heard that before." Gunny took a breath, tipping his chin up, staring into the darkness overhead. "*Jesus*."

"The fuck you talking about?" Brute ran his comment back through his mind, not finding anything to cause this reaction.

"Never heard you laugh, brother. Sounds good, man. Sounds real good. Looks good on ya, too. Brute's Girl changed your life."

Fuck.

Brute didn't respond, just turned to look at where Bexley sat. She was peering across the yard in a different direction, a wide grin on her face, and Brute twisted so he could see what she was looking at.

Fuck.

Tequila, one of the chapter's officers, stood with his shoulders against a tree, looking down at Natty, who was staring up at him. From the grin on Tequila's face, he must have just made a joke, but from the look on Natty's, he might as well have hung the moon.

"Fuck."

BEXLEY

Leaning her shoulders against the trunk of the spreading oak tree, Bexley looked out at the occupants of the park. Joggers, dog walkers, cyclists, babysitters, basketball players—everyone here seemed to have a thing they were intent on doing. There were only a couple of people who were like her. Sitters. Watchers. Relaxers. *I could make up words*, she thought with a silent laugh. *Waitingers. Lingereroli*. Head back, she let the sun blind her for a moment, dappling down through the leaves. Eyes closed, bright splotches lighting up the darkness behind her lids, Bexley did what she had done so many times as she sat in this exact spot. She listened.

Excited whines accompanied the carefully paced thuds of a runner and his dog. The thud, pause, thud, pause from the direction of the basketball court signaled an imminent free throw. She sorted through the sounds, waiting.

Never soon enough, but it wasn't long before she heard it. The rumble that could be felt as well as heard. Sometimes it had approached, at times retreated, and now she knew what it was. Nervously, she smoothed down her skirt, eyes still closed, still listening. Louder and louder, echoing off the buildings and trees until the trunk behind her vibrated with the sound. The silence, when it came, was startling. Gradually, the park came back to life, sounds filling in the empty spaces, accompanied by the fall of footsteps approaching from her left, where the parking lot was.

Tipping her head, she opened her eyes and looked up into the face of the man she loved. "Hey." She smiled at him, thinking the words, not caring when they fell from her lips instead. "Your eyes are so beautiful." Brute crouched next to her, reaching out to draw her close, brushing his lips against hers. Doc B, as she called Bulldog, had worked miracles to ease Brute's pain over the past year, which meant when he smiled back at her, it was a full-on quirk of his lips, not just the small movements and expressions she'd gotten used to at first. "You told me once I was your dream."

With a teasing laugh, he settled to the ground next to her, hip-to-hip, facing her as he leaned across on one arm. "You are." He bent close and kissed her again. "Always, Bex." His other hand gripped her elbow for a moment, then slipped up to her shoulder, tugging the neckline of her shirt slightly sideways so he could press his lips to her collarbone. He dragged a soft kiss across the words there, simple script in Latin that read *Amor vitae meae*. Her only tattoo, a surprise for his birthday three months ago, and one he still found delight in. "Love of my life."

"Why did you want to meet here, Brute?" They were going to dinner later with friends. Ruby had secured a pair of babysitters, necessary for two sets of twins who were both mobile and inquisitive. So Slate and Ruby, Gunny and Sharon, and Brute and Bexley would be meeting at the local Italian restaurant for an evening of fun and food. "I love it here. I used to come and sit, just reading, for the longest time. So peaceful."

"I know." A smile she'd come to love danced across his features. "I watched you."

Tell him? She grinned, reaching up to thread her fingers through his, feeding his words back to him. "I know." Laughing aloud at his honest shock, she told him, "Your bike isn't exactly quiet, you know." Now he was laughing and shaking his head. "I didn't know who you were then, of course. Didn't know why that biker was here so often to just park and sit. Not until I saw you on my street that day."

She and Brute had talked about the Sunday that had seen the Rebel column ride in front of her house. The first time she'd met Gunny she'd thanked him in the only way she knew. Brute had grinned at Gunny's helpless pose, elbows lifted to shoulder level, trying not to touch Bexley anywhere as she wrapped her arms around his chest and hugged tightly. His growl of, "Get your girl off me, brother," had made Brute laugh, too. She smoothed her skirt again, fingers toying with the fabric for a moment.

A lot of things made him laugh these days, and she loved the sound each time it graced the air around her.

"I can't tell you the number of times I dreamed of this, sweetheart." Laughter dying away, he stared at her intently, his features softening in a way she loved. Bexley shivered as his thumb traced across the words on her skin again. "Wishing for the right to cross the green to sit beside you. To talk to you, ask you what you were reading, kiss you in the sunlight." Matching actions to words, he leaned in and pressed his lips to hers. "Wanted to ask you something, thought this was the right place."

"Brute." She started to offer reassurances, but he shook his head.

"You need to know, honey." Deep breath in and he held it a moment before blowing it out in a rush. "You know where I was."

He'd gotten home last night, late. She'd picked him up at the airport after he'd got off the last plane of the day coming in from Chicago and points west. She knew his flight out had gone straight to Portland. There for three days, she didn't know the why of that leg to her hometown, but the important part was on his return trip. She knew he had a detour on his way back, had intentionally booked a layover in Salt Lake of a day. They hadn't talked about it before he'd left, but she knew. It had been a long time coming, but Chief, whoever the somber sounding stranger on the phone was, had finally come through.

Tugging, she brought their joined hands to her mouth, pressing his knuckles to her lips. It didn't matter what those hands had done. "Never leaving you." Another kiss, this one hard, her eyes dipping closed. "Not going anywhere, Brute." His hand tightened around her fingers. "I waited for you for so long." His mouth was on hers, not soft, not questing, this kiss demanded her surrender, and she opened as his tongue thrust inside, sweeping and tangling with hers. Hand released, she twined her arms around his neck, pulling him close even as he gripped her hips and shifted her towards him. They broke apart, and he pressed his forehead to hers, lips still touching, sharing each breath.

"I love you, Bexley."

BRUTE

He sat, mug in hand, watching the strolling residents passing to and fro in front of their cottage. Lifting a hand to this one, giving a tip of his head to the next, he sipped his coffee and leaned against the wall. The changes in his life were astounding. Two years ago he would have been holed up in his apartment, shades drawn, headset on to answer customer service questions, working overtime because he had nothing more important in his life.

Today was filled with plans, and his had begun an hour earlier when he woke Bexley up in what had become his favorite way. Kissing along her shoulder to her neck, up to her cheek where he used gentle kisses to spell out his promise to her. *Mine. Always. Forever.*

He tracked her progress through the house by her footsteps. Back and forth from their bedroom to the bathroom, then a side trip to his office, where she didn't think he knew about the stash of tiny boxes, each with the embossed logo of a local baby boutique. A wish not yet voiced, but he'd be ready when she was.

Another barefoot pass up the hallway to their bedroom, and her soft padding footsteps were replaced by the confident clip of her heels as she came down the stairs.

"Brute?" She called him as if they lived in a mansion and he might be wandering through the west wing in search of something. Shaking his head in amusement, he reached out and thumped a fist against the wall. A moment later, the door opened, and she peered around the edge, blue eyes smiling at him. "There you are." Spoken with as much relief as if she'd been searching for hours, only now stumbling on him.

"Here I am." He agreed with her and lifted the nearly empty cup. "Needed some coffee, honey. Come sit with me." Rounding the edge of the door, she reached out and took the mug, gripping his hand with her other one. The bright colors of her strapless sundress blazed in the sunlight.

"We're going to be late."

She gave his hand a sharp tug, and he watched mesmerized as a ringlet tumbled free from the complicated mass of curls pinned to the top of her head. He was going to enjoy taking that down later, liking her best when her hair was free, swirling around her beautiful face. Or when it was braided into two pigtails, her chin leaning on his shoulder as they rode the bike down country roads. Or when it was tied back in a ponytail, swept out of the way so she could dive for a ball thrown by her nephew. *Our nephew*.

"Not like they can start without us, sweetheart." Cradling her hand in his, he pulled her close, loving how she came to him confidently, chin raised so her head tipped back, giving him easy access to her mouth. "Give me my coffee back."

From her grin, he knew she was going to take the bait, and he smiled down at her as she played her part. "What'll you give me for it?"

Those sparkling blue eyes staring up at him, she lifted her lips, waiting. Without hesitation, he answered as he always did, as he had done since the first time he saw her. Two words that tied them together so much more than the ones which would be spoken later today. They didn't need an "I do" repeated after a preacher to bring them closer. All it took was, "A kiss."

~ Fini ~

THANK YOU FOR READING
A Kiss to Keep You!

Love will find a way, and for Brute and Bexley it comes to life standing under the bright lights of a grocery store aisle. 'A Kiss to Keep You' is a short, sweet, happily ever after story that I hope you adore as much as I did. Loved writing this story, and the emotions are so real. To learn more about Slate and Ruby, as well as Gunny and other members of the Rebel Wayfarers MC, you should read the series.

ABOUT THE AUTHOR

Raised in the south, MariaLisa learned about the magic of books at an early age. Every summer, she would spend hours in the local library, devouring books of every genre. Self-described as a book-a-holic, she says "I've always loved to read, but then I discovered writing, and found I adored that, too. For reading...if nothing else is available, I've been known to read the back of the cereal box."

Also by MariaLisa deMora

Alace Sweets

A dark thriller, this book is not a light read. Filled with edge-of-your-seat suspense, this intense story commands the reader's attention as it drives towards the explosive ending. Alace Sweets is a vigilante serial killer, with everything that implies and is sure to trip all your triggers. Be ready.

At seventeen, Alace Sweets turned a corner in her life, taking the wrong shortcut home from school.

Resisting the harsh knowledge her attackers will never be made to pay for their actions, Alace takes a stand. Justice must be served, and if fate's scales are out of balance, she's determined to set things right as best she can.

When the laws of men fail, the rules of Alace prevail.

5-Star Reviews for Alace Sweets

"deMora has a superb story-line and exceptional character development. All of her characters have such depth that will intrigue the reader..."
~Turning Another Page

"Hot, sweet, dark thriller."
~Beth D

"It will keep you on the edge of your seat and give you chills."
~Escape Reality Book Blog

"Disturbing, haunting, sickly; yet hot, sexy and heart racing!"
~Amanda L

"From the first page [deMora] pulls you into the world she has created and you do not even try to escape..."
~Little Shop of Readers Blog

"A must read for all those dark, gritty romance fans out there."
~Sweet & Spicy Reads

"You will find yourself so drawn into the story that the outside world is blocked out and your locking the doors and turning on all the lights."
~Danena F

"Don't judge me for bonding with a vigilante serial killer, she's more than what she does."
~iScream Books

"Thrilling...chilling...full of suspense, nail biting edge of your seat excitement."
~Tracey H

"Every time MariaLisa deMora picks up her pen (or opens her computer), she creates characters you want to believe in."
~Gail S

"Intriguing dark storyline, beautiful love story and nail-biting conclusion, what more could a reader ask for?"
~Manda M

"This book takes you a dark and twisted ride that is gripping..."
~Renee Entress' Blog

"This book is dark and gritty and I literally had to take a day off from reading it because it's that intense."
~My Girlfriend's Couch

"This is my favourite book so far from this author ... I recommend this book if you enjoy dark romantic thrillers."
~Cheekypee Reads and Reviews

"There's not enough stars to give this book and 5 just doesn't really do it justice!"
~DeLane C

"I couldn't put this book down from page one! Tried to stop & go to bed but couldn't sleep thinking about Alace and got up & finished the book."
~Debbie M

"MariaLisa DeMora, wordsmith that she is, made this a story of the enlightenment of a woman and finding love in a life where she has had none."
~Kat W

"Whatever deep dark trench [deMora] pulled a character like Alace from should be revisited again and often."
~Confessions of a Serial Reader

ADDITIONAL SERIES AND BOOKS

Please note that books in a series frequently feature characters from additional books within that series. If series books are read out of order, readers will twig to spoilers for the other books, so going back to read the skipped titles won't have the same angsty reveals.

Rebel Wayfarers MC series:

Mica, #1
A Sweet & Merry Christmas, short story #1.5
Slate, #2
Bear, #3
Jase, #4
Gunny, #5
Mason, #6
Hoss, #7
Harddrive Holidays, short story #7.5
Duck, #8
Biker Chick Campout, short story #8.5
Watcher, #9
A Kiss to Keep You, novella #9.25
Gun Totin' Annie, short story #9.5
Secret Santa, short story #9.75
Bones, #10
Gunny's Pups, novella #10.25
Never Settle, short story #10.5
Not Even A Mouse, short story #10.75
Fury, #11
Christmas Doings, #11.25
Gypsy's Lady, #11.5
Cassie, #12
Road Runner's Ride, novella #12.5

Occupy Yourself band series:

Born Into Trouble, #1
Grace In Motion, #2 (TBD)
What They Say, #3 (TBD)

Neither This, Nor That series:

This Is the Route Of Twisted Pain, #1
Treading the Traitor's Path: Out Bad, #2
Trapped by Fate on Reckless Roads, #3 (TBD)

Other Books:

With My Whole Heart
Alace Sweets
Hard Focus

More information available at mldemora.com.